# Eagle Eight
## Into the Breach

ISBN: 979-8-9928626-0-7 (Paperback)
979-8-9928626-1-4 (eBook)

# DEDICATION:

For my girls Erika and Emma. May all your dreams come true.

Mrs Zaglewski, my freshman year English Comp professor made me work for that "C". The way you pushed me to be better, made me who I am today as a writer. After reading this book she may want to reconsider being so generous with that letter grade. *It is a good thing final grades are in and can't be changed.*

# CHAPTER 1

## HOME

Whistling to himself, Chris stepped out of the jewelry store, slipping the small velvet box into his pocket. The sun was blinding, and he squinted as his gaze settled on Jody—his best friend—standing by the theater entrance. He wasn't alone. A tall, slender brunette stood close to him, her face partially obscured by the sunlight.

Chris froze in place.

Jody tucked the woman's long hair behind her ear, pulling her closer. The two embraced, Jody's hands trailing along her waist, his touch familiar, intimate.

Chris took a step forward, his breath quickening.

Then, the brunette shifted slightly, giving him a clear view of her face.

Suzy.

His Suzy.

His body locked up. His mind refused to process what he was seeing. The world around him blurred as his vision tunneled in on the two of them.

His hand clenched around the tiny velvet box in his pocket. Rage surged through him.

"What the hell?!"

His voice slammed through the air, sharp and raw.

A few heads turned. Jody and Suzy snapped apart, their eyes darting toward him.

Chris locked eyes with Suzy. Her expression flashed with panic. For a split second, she looked like she might run—but then, the crowd around them began to grow, people murmuring, slowing their steps to watch.

Suzy ducked her head and disappeared into the gathering onlookers, pressing herself between strangers, hoping to vanish into the sea of faces.

Chris barely registered her retreat. His focus was on Jody now.

His feet carried him forward. His breath came in ragged bursts.

Jody's mouth opened like he wanted to explain— like there was any possible excuse.

Chris didn't let him. He buried his shoulder into Jody's chest, slamming him back against the brick wall. The force of the impact knocked the air from Jody's lungs in a sharp oof.

For a split second, Chris thought he had him.

Then, Jody retaliated.

His elbow drove into Chris's back, breaking the hold. Chris staggered, and in an instant, Jody drove his knee up into his stomach, shoving him backward. Before Chris could regain his balance, a fist smashed into his face.

Pain exploded in his mouth. His cheek split against his teeth, filling his mouth with the sharp taste of blood and betrayal.

Chris hit the pavement hard, breathless. His vision blurred at the edges. His ears rang with the rush of white-hot rage and the distant gasps of the crowd.

Someone muttered, "Holy shit."

Jody stood over him, fists clenched, breathing heavily. His jaw was tight, but there wasn't an ounce of regret in his face.

Chris wiped the blood from his mouth, his hands trembling with fury. His eyes burned as he forced himself to look up at the person he had once called a brother.

"How could you do this to me?"

Jody snorted, shaking his head. "Fuck you. You're the one abandoning us. Running off to the military, leaving everything behind like we don't matter." His voice was thick with anger. "You think you're better than us, Chris? Well, guess what? Suzy's with me now. And you can take your high-and-mighty bullshit and shove it."

Chris barely breathed as Jody turned and walked away.

And somewhere in the crowd, Suzy was still there. Watching. Hiding.

Chris clenched his jaw. She wasn't worth looking for.

Not anymore.

***

Chris didn't remember getting up. One minute, he was on the pavement. The next, he was moving through the mall, aimless, his feet carrying him on autopilot.

His cheek throbbed. His fists were still clenched.

At some point, he stopped.

The recruiter's office.

The bold AIR FORCE sign gleamed under the fluorescent lights. Before he could second-guess himself, he threw the door open.

A man in a blue uniform sat at a single desk, the stripes on his sleeve marking him as a Staff Sergeant. He looked up, startled, then smiled.

"Mr. Tanner. Wasn't expecting you today. What brings you in?"

Chris's chest heaved. His voice came out hoarse. "Sergeant Vossmer, I know my enlistment isn't for a couple more months, but...I need out. Now."

The recruiter's expression shifted. "What happened?"

Chris swallowed hard. His throat felt raw.

"I just saw my best friend making out with my girlfriend."

A pause. Then, Vossmer exhaled through his nose, nodding like he'd seen this before.

"You leave now, you'll lose your job assignment. You'll come in open contract—could end up anywhere."

Chris barely hesitated. "I don't care."

Vossmer studied him for a moment, then nodded. "I can make it happen. You ship out tomorrow morning."

Chris tapped his foot impatiently as the sergeant prepared the paperwork.

When the contract was slid across the desk, along with a pen, Vossmer leaned in slightly.

"Listen, son. Do you think running solves anything? It doesn't. You leave town, but your problems don't disappear." He tapped the paper. "You sign this, you'd better be ready to step up. Because those who let emotions control them? They don't last."

Chris clenched his jaw. Without another word, he signed.

Vossmer gave him a firm handshake. And just like that, his old life was gone.

***

Chris drove home on autopilot. His hands ached from gripping the steering wheel too hard. His shirt was damp from tears he didn't even remember shedding.

He barely remembered climbing the porch steps, slamming the front door, or shouting, "Mom!"

She was at the dining table, laptop open, a cup of coffee in her hands. She blinked up at him, startled.

"Chris? What's wrong?"

He ran a hand through his hair, pacing. His heart still hammered against his ribs.

"I just saw Jody and Suzy outside the theater." His voice cracked. "They were all over each other."

His mother's face softened. "Oh, honey. I'm so sorry."

Chris let out a harsh, bitter laugh. "I knew Jody was sneaking around with someone. I just never thought—" He stopped. His hands shook as he pulled the small velvet box from his pocket and flipped it open.

The diamond inside glinted under the kitchen light.

"Shit," he muttered. "I was going to ask her to marry me this weekend."

His mother sighed. "Sweetheart, when one door closes, another—"

"Don't give me that bullshit."

She flinched. Chris exhaled sharply, shaking his head. His pulse pounded in his ears.

Then, before he could stop himself, he ripped his car keys from his pocket, along with the ring box, and tossed them onto the table.

"Here. Take them. Do whatever you want. I don't give a damn. Donate it to your fucking church if you want."

His mother stared at him, speechless.

Chris straightened his spine. "I'm leaving. I spoke to the recruiter. I ship out tomorrow."

A heavy silence filled the air.

Finally, his mother nodded slowly. "I see."

Chris turned on his heel, marching toward his room.

He didn't look back.

# CHAPTER 2

## MEPS

The wind cut through Chris's thin jacket, sending a sharp chill down his spine. He clenched his fists inside his pockets, not out of anger this time, but to keep the blood flowing.

Around him, the murmuring group of recruits stood huddled against the cold, their faces a mix of excitement, exhaustion, and quiet anxiety. Some rocked on their heels to stay warm, others stared blankly at the ground, waiting.

At exactly 5:00 AM, the door to the Military Entrance Processing Station swung open.

A man in uniform stepped outside, his boots grinding against the pavement as he came to a halt in front of them. He didn't look tired. He didn't look cold. He looked pissed off.

"Listen up!" his voice cut through the pre-dawn air like a whip.

"You will form a single-file line against the building. No outside food or drinks—trash them now. You'll take a mouthpiece from the bin, attach it to the breathalyzer, and blow until it beeps. Fail? You're gone. Pass? Go inside, state your branch, last name first, and get your nametag. Keep it above your left breast.

No talking. No screwing around. Do you understand?"

A garbled chorus of "Yes, sir!" rang out.

Chris fell into line, his body running on autopilot. He followed each step as instructed, taking a mouthpiece, blowing into the breathalyzer, waiting for the beep. His breath was steady, but his mind wasn't.

The machine beeped.

Chris removed the mouthpiece, trashed it, and stepped inside.

*\*\**

The waiting room felt like a high school classroom, complete with uncomfortable chairs and too many rules. Chris sat, nametag stuck to his chest, watching as people were called one by one.

Army. Marine Corps. Navy. Air Force. Even Coast Guard.

A rotating door of uniforms appeared, calling names and escorting recruits down the halls. The room emptied slowly. But Chris remained seated.

He checked the clock. Two hours had passed.

A flicker of unease crept into his gut. What the hell was the holdup?

Finally, the door opened, and a woman in Air Force blue stepped inside. But she wasn't enlisted—she was an officer.

Captain.

Her silver bars glinted under the fluorescent lights, the parallel railroad tracks of a USAF Captain.

She scanned the room, her gaze sharp.

"Tanner, Christopher. Come with me."

\*\*\*

Chris followed Captain Scott through a maze of sterile hallways, his footsteps barely audible against the polished floors. The farther they went, the quieter it became.

"Mr. Tanner," she said, her tone neutral, unreadable. "I'm Captain Alison Scott. I have a few things to discuss with you."

"Yes, ma'am," Chris responded automatically.

At the end of the hall, they stopped at a plain office door, a black nameplate marking it as hers:

## CPT. A. SCOTT – USAF

She pushed the door open, revealing an immaculate office. Minimalist. Cold. A desk with only the essentials—a lamp, a nameplate, a single framed photo on the back wall.

The photo showed a massive plane, its silhouette striking against the sky.

"Take a seat," she said, motioning to the chair across from her.

Chris sat.

Scott took her place behind the desk, flipping open a thick folder.

Chris recognized his own photo clipped to the front. But something felt off. The grainy image was not recent. His hair was longer, darker. It looked like it had been taken from a distance—and then enlarged.

Chris's stomach tightened.

Scott flipped through pages, occasionally scribbling notes. The silence stretched.

Then, finally—

"Mr. Tanner. Six foot one and three quarters. One hundred and eighty-nine pounds."

"Yes, ma'am."

"Were you a wrestler in school?"

"No, ma'am. I played football for a couple of years."

Scott nodded, jotting something down. "Three years ROTC. Reached the rank of Cadet Major."

"Yes, ma'am."

She paused, studying him. "Majored in Aerospace Engineering. Minored in Environmental Engineering."

Chris swallowed. How much did she know?

"Yes, ma'am."

"And you authored a paper titled Evidence-Based Rehabilitation of Microclimates."

Chris stiffened. That paper wasn't common knowledge.

He blinked, trying to mask his confusion. "Yes… but that was just an academic project."

Scott leaned back, twisting her pen between her fingers.

"Mr. Tanner, you weren't scheduled to be here for a couple more months. Why did you hasten your arrival?"

Chris hesitated.

He could lie. But he had the sinking suspicion she already knew the answer.

"My home life has fallen apart," he admitted. "My father left years ago. My mother buried herself in church." He exhaled, jaw tight. "My best friend and my girlfriend are… together now."

Scott nodded slowly, as if confirming something she already suspected.

She jotted something else down, then set the pen aside and folded her hands.

Her next words sent an icy chill through him.

"Mr. Tanner," she said, voice carefully measured, "can you completely sever your ties to home?"

Chris frowned. "You mean, like… not visit?"

Scott's eyes didn't waver.

"Not visit. Not write. Not call. Not even acknowledge them."

The air thickened.

Chris shifted in his seat. "I… don't understand."

Scott leaned forward, just slightly. "If you walk out of here today, your past life ceases to exist. Permanently."

Chris's throat felt dry. His mind reeled. This wasn't normal enlistment talk. Something else was happening.

Scott continued, unshaken.

"You will be expected to operate at the highest level of confidentiality. Any attempt to contact someone from your previous life—even your mother—will be considered a breach of national security."

She paused. Then, just as casually as if discussing the weather, she added:

"And it will be punishable under the Uniform Code of Military Justice. Maximum penalty…"

A slight tilt of her head.

"Death."

Chris's pulse pounded. For the first time since arriving, fear crept into his gut. He opened his mouth—then closed it. His brain scrambled for an explanation, a loophole, anything.

But Scott wasn't bluffing.

The realization slammed into him like a freight train. This wasn't just the Air Force. It was something else entirely.

He took a slow, steadying breath.

Then, finally, he nodded.

"Yes, ma'am."

Scott didn't smile.

She simply turned a thick form toward him and pointed.

"Sign at the bottom. Initial here. After you complete OCS, you'll receive further details about your assignment."

Chris stared at the pen in his hand. A signature. A few marks on a page. That was all it took to erase everything. His mother. His past. His entire life.

His fingers tightened around the pen.

This is it.

He pressed the tip to the paper.

And signed.

# CHAPTER 3

## PT

The thunderous banging on his dorm room door sent shockwaves through Chris Tanner's skull.

Tanner jolted awake—disoriented, heart hammering, breath uneven. For a split second, he didn't know where he was.

Then it hit him.

Zero four hundred hours.

Shit.

He scrambled out of bed, his brain still lagging behind his body as he lunged for the door. The second it swung open, he was met with the blinding fluorescent glare of the hallway and the shuffling forms of exhausted cadets standing stiffly against the walls.

Puffy-eyed. Stiff-backed. Barely awake.

A swarm of senior cadets buzzed through the hall, barking orders, barely pausing as they moved from one poor soul to the next.

"Stand up straight! Heels together! Toes at a forty-five-degree angle! Thumbs on the seam of your trousers! Move like you've got a purpose!"

Tanner stiffened automatically, his ROTC muscle memory kicking in before his brain could fully register it. Then came the first real shock of the morning.

From somewhere down the hall, an upperclassman's voice exploded.

"Oh, you've gotta be shitting me!"

The hallway went dead silent.

Tanner caught movement as another senior cadet rushed over, took one look at whatever nightmare was unfolding, and let out a barking laugh.

"Collins! Get your ass over here! You are NOT gonna believe this!"

Tanner didn't dare move, but his curiosity burned.

Heavy boots stomped down the hall. The upperclassman stopped short, then immediately threw up a hand to shield his view.

"Jesus Christ! Nature Boy, what the hell were you thinking?!"

The cadet in question—completely naked, except for a stunned expression—stood frozen, his body at rigid attention.

"Oh my god!" The senior cadet wheeled around to block his view, shielding his eyes with one hand while pointing wildly with the other. "Your one-eyed copilot is standing at better attention than you are!"

Stifled snorts and muffled laughter rippled through the hallway.

The naked cadet swallowed hard, his face redder than a warning light.

"I—I lost my towel, sir!"

"Lost your towel?!" The senior cadet threw his arms in the air. "So you decided the best course of action was to parade your goddamn birthday suit through MY hallway?!"

The cadet squeaked out a pitiful "Yes, sir."

The upperclassman sighed dramatically, then jabbed a finger toward the door.

"Get your ass back in your room and PUT SOME DAMN CLOTHES ON! Now!"

"Yes, sir!" The unfortunate cadet bolted back into his room, the door slamming shut behind him.

The hall was still like a graveyard—except for the barely contained snickers.

"The rest of you—eyes forward!" The upperclassman barked. "Unless you wanna join Nature Boy in his fashion statement!"

The laughter died immediately.

***

Tanner stood ramrod straight, the adrenaline still buzzing through his veins.

Then—warm breath against his ear. A soft voice, eerily gentle.

"Good morning, sleepyhead… it's time to—"

The whisper morphed into a full-volume explosion.

"WAKE THE FUCK UP!"

Tanner's eyes snapped open, his body jerking violently upright.

Shit.

Had he…?

His stomach dropped. He'd been standing at attention—asleep.

The upperclassman leaned in close, their face inches from his own.

Tanner barely had time to process before they stepped back and shouted to the entire group.

"Perhaps a couple of miles will wake him up! In fact—maybe ALL of us could use a morning run!"

Groans rippled through the cadets, but no one dared protest.

The upperclassman's eyes locked onto Tanner.

"Lead us out Sleeping Beauty! Form up downstairs!"

Tanner swallowed hard. He knew what was coming. Without a word, he took off down the hall, pushing past the others toward the stairwell—

And was slammed into the doorframe.

Hard.

Pain shot through his shoulder as he stumbled sideways. He barely had time to recover before a voice—low and venomous—hissed at him.

A classmate. A glare full of hate.

Tanner barely had time to register the hostility before the kid moved on, blending into the crowd.

What the hell was that about? No time to think about it.

PT was waiting.

\*\*\*

The next several hours were a blur of agony. Running. Miles upon miles. The pavement pounded beneath his boots, lungs burning, legs screaming.

Push-ups. His arms trembled, sweat dripped onto the pavement, and elbows buckled with every rep.

Sit-ups. Their core was on fire, breath ragged, every crunch sending waves of pain through his gut.

Mountain climbers. Their knees slammed into his chest, thighs screaming for mercy.

And then—the burpees.

Tanner had never known true evil until that moment.

A sadistic fusion of push-ups and jumping jacks, designed by someone with a personal vendetta against the human body.

Every muscle in his body screamed for relief.

And yet—every few minutes—

A sharp elbow to his ribs.

Tanner gritted his teeth, eyes flicking sideways.

Same guy. Same hostile glare.

Tanner didn't know his name. Didn't know why he had a problem. But it wasn't over.

Not by a long shot.

# CHAPTER 4

## THE RUCK MARCH FROM HELL

The sky was still a deep black, stars barely flickering through the heavy clouds. Tanner stood in formation with the rest of the cadets, ruck strapped tight to his back, rifle slung across his chest. The weight dug into his shoulders, pressing his boots deeper into the damp earth.

"Move out!"

The command cut through the morning silence, and like a lumbering war machine, the cadets started marching.

One step. Then another. Miles stretched endlessly ahead.

Tanner focused on his breathing, his legs falling into rhythm with the steady thud-thud-thud of boots against dirt.

The weight was suffocating. His back ached, muscles burned, and the damp chill sank into his bones.

At first, the pace was manageable.

Then it picked up.

The drill instructors barked orders from the sides, their voices sharp in the cold air.

"Faster! If you fall behind, you'll be dragging your entire squad down with you!"

The road turned rougher, steeper. Sweat dripped down Tanner's spine, soaking his shirt beneath the heavy gear. His lungs pulled harder for air.

Then—movement up ahead.

A cadet—one of the smaller guys, barely making pace—was pushed.

Tanner saw it happen.

A deliberate shove. Not hard enough to be obvious, but strong enough that the guy's exhausted legs couldn't recover.

The cadet stumbled forward, his knees buckling beneath the weight of his ruck. His hands flew out, but it was too late—he hit the dirt hard.

Tanner's stomach twisted.

He didn't need to guess who did it.

As the fallen cadet struggled, boots stomped past him without a second glance.

And just ahead, looking smug as hell, was the same asshole who'd slammed into Tanner at PT.

The rival glanced over his shoulder, met Tanner's stare, and smirked.

Tanner's fists clenched.

The formation kept moving. The smaller cadet wasn't getting up. His ruck was too heavy, pinning him down.

Tanner hesitated.

Help him, or follow orders?

"KEEP MOVING!" the instructor bellowed.

Tanner clenched his jaw, then shifted his weight and grabbed the fallen cadet's pack.

"On your feet, man!" he hissed.

The cadet gasped, eyes wide, but pulled himself up with Tanner's help.

The moment cost precious seconds—Tanner's heart slammed in his chest as he jogged to catch up. His legs screamed in protest.

Ahead, his rival watched the whole thing unfold.

"How noble, Tanner," the guy muttered under his breath as Tanner pulled alongside him. "Hope that kindness doesn't get you killed one day."

Tanner's jaw locked. He saw what you did, you piece of shit. But there was no proof. If he called him out now, it would be his word against nothing.

The weight was unbearable now. His ruck felt like it had doubled in size, pressing harder and harder onto his spine. His muscles screamed for relief.

By the time they reached the checkpoint, Tanner's legs were on fire, his arms numb from the weight.

The drill instructor took one look at him, then at the weaker cadet he helped.

"Tanner! You wanna be a hero? Fine."

The instructor pointed to a sandbag.

"Pick that up. Carry it the rest of the way."

Tanner's stomach dropped.

Another fifty pounds. Added to his already breaking body.

He bent down, heaved it up. His spine screamed.

As the march continued, his rival walked past, slow, deliberate, his smirk widening.

"Great job, Captain America."

Tanner bit down his anger.

This was going to be hell.

# CHAPTER 5

## THE DROWN-PROOFING TEST

Tanner's feet hit the icy water, and immediately, his lungs clenched. The shock sent a violent shudder through his body, but he bit down the instinct to panic.

Hands tied behind his back. Ankles bound together.

Survive.

That was the only rule.

The pool stretched dark and endless beneath him. Candidates thrashed around him, some bobbing, some sinking.

Tanner took a deep breath.

Tilt forward. Let yourself fall.

The moment his body hit the water, it was fight or die.

His heart pounded in his skull, his arms and legs struggling against their bindings.

The technique had been drilled into him before—duck under, propel up, catch a breath.

He managed it once. Then again.

Then someone splashed violently beside him.

A cadet—one of the bigger guys—was thrashing, gasping for air.

Tanner glanced over. His gut tightened.

Then—another sharp splash.

Tanner saw a pair of boots kick out—right into the drowning cadet's stomach. A deliberate kick.

Tanner whipped his head around just in time to see his rival's face—neutral, focused—but with the same smugness as before.

The drowning cadet sank beneath the surface.

Tanner's stomach flipped.

That wasn't an accident. The guy had been struggling, but staying afloat—until the kick sent him under.

Tanner had seconds to decide. Ignore him and survive? Or help and risk drowning?

"Slow your breathing! Move with the water, not against it!" Tanner hissed through clenched teeth, jerking his head toward the drowning cadet.

But the guy was panicking.

Tanner had to act.

He kicked toward him, tilting his weight just enough to shoulder-bump him upright.

"Follow my movement! Stop fighting it!" Tanner gritted out, lungs burning.

The cadet's eyes were wild, but he mimicked Tanner's motion.

The instructor's whistle cut through the air.

Another splash—a safety swimmer yanked the struggling cadet out of the water, dragging him to the edge.

Tanner barely caught his own breath before a sharp voice rang out.

"You trying to be a damn lifeguard, Tanner?"

Tanner snapped his head up. The instructor was staring directly at him. Tanner said nothing, chest still heaving.

The instructor smirked.

"Next time, I'll give you a boat anchor instead. See how much of a hero you feel then."

A few cadets chuckled.

Tanner's jaw locked.

And just beyond the instructor's gaze, his rival smirked, his expression all too satisfied.

Tanner knew exactly what had happened. The bastard had targeted someone weaker again—just like the ruck march. And worse? Tanner had reacted.

Which meant the instructor noticed. Which meant the rival had won this round.

Tanner clenched his jaw and forced himself to stay still.

The test wasn't over.

And he wasn't about to sink because of that son of a bitch

# CHAPTER 6

## ACADEMICS

The classroom was stiflingly hot, filled with the faint scent of burnt coffee and ink-stained hands. Tanner sat at a desk covered in maps, tactical reports, and mission briefings, trying to keep his brain from melting out of his ears.

Across from him, the instructor—a stone-faced Captain with zero patience for hesitation—pointed at the map on the projector screen.

"Candidate Tanner. Your convoy has been ambushed. You have four wounded, two vehicles disabled, and hostiles moving to encircle your position. What do you do?"

Tanner blinked fast, trying to push past the fog in his brain. He was running on fumes after a week of endless training, drills, and tests.

He glanced at the map. Think.

"Sir, I'd establish a defensive perimeter with the remaining vehicles, use suppressive fire to buy time for a medevac request, and—"

"Wrong."

The Captain's voice cut like a blade.

Tanner clenched his jaw. Wrong?!

"You're assuming you have time for medevac. You don't. Your radio's been jammed. Next option?"

Tanner's mind raced, flipping through the strategies he had drilled into his head.

"Sir, I'd order the least-injured men to carry the wounded while the rest of the unit provides covering fire. We move toward the nearest defensible structure."

The Captain stared at him. Beat.

Then:

"Acceptable."

Tanner exhaled, tension leaking from his shoulders.

"But next time, don't assume you have reinforcements coming. You're alone. Act like it."

Tanner nodded, but inside, he was screaming. This was just the first class of the day.

And it wasn't going to get easier.

***

By the time he made it to the next session, Tanner's brain felt fried.

The legal instructor—an older Major with a voice like sandpaper—paced in front of the room, flipping through slides of case studies, rules of engagement, and ethical dilemmas.

Tanner took notes as fast as he could, but the words were starting to blur together.

Then came the question that shook him awake.

"Candidate Tanner. You are leading a squad on a classified mission. During the operation, you capture a high-value enemy target. He knows where an IED is set to detonate within the hour. He refuses to talk."

The Major turned, leveling Tanner with a cold, unreadable stare.

"How do you handle the situation?"

Tanner hesitated.

The answer should have been simple. But it wasn't.

He glanced at the Geneva Convention section in his notes, knowing the obvious, legal answer.

But what if it was his team on the line?

What if people died because he followed the book?

"Sir... I would utilize psychological pressure tactics to extract the information, but I would not violate rules of engagement or human rights laws."

The Major didn't flinch.

"And if your hesitation costs lives?"

Tanner's stomach knotted.

He took a steady breath. "Sir, I would exhaust every legal means possible before resorting to unlawful coercion."

The Major held his stare, then nodded.

"Good. But remember, Lieutenant, in the field, moral dilemmas don't come with a textbook answer."

Tanner gripped his pen tighter.

Like he needed more pressure.

***

By midmorning, Tanner was running on caffeine fumes, struggling through an advanced engineering course on ballistics, explosive ordinance disposal, and tactical infrastructure.

The instructor—a hard-nosed Lieutenant Colonel with a background in demolitions—grinned as he wrote a formula on the board.

"Alright, candidates, pop quiz: If you have two pounds of C-4 and need to take down a steel-reinforced door without causing structural collapse, what's the correct charge placement and detonation sequence?"

Tanner stared at the board like it had personally betrayed him.

Explosives weren't his specialty—that was more of an EOD thing, and he was an aerospace guy.

But failure wasn't an option.

His mind fought through the exhaustion, pulling up bits and pieces of lessons from past training.

He scribbled down:

- Shaped charge, directed force at door frame.
- Time delay to minimize risk.
- Blast wave focused outward to avoid secondary collapse.

The instructor glanced over his work.

Then nodded.

Tanner let out a breath. One step closer to surviving the day.

***

The final class of the day was where Tanner's exhaustion truly caught up to him.

The instructor—a sharp-eyed intelligence officer with a background in psychological warfare—gave them one task:

Break your opponent without firing a shot.

Tanner was paired against another candidate, both given identical mission profiles—one defending a position, the other trying to gain access through deception, intimidation, or manipulation.

Tanner took the offensive role.

His opponent was stronger, smarter, and dead-set on resisting.

So Tanner went a different route.

"They already sold you out, you know."

His opponent's brow twitched.

"Your team. They left you here. They didn't even radio for backup."

No reaction.

Tanner tilted his head, pretending to check his watch.

"Funny thing about patience. The longer we sit here, the more time my guys have to dismantle your defenses. Hell, maybe they already have."

A flicker of doubt.

Tanner leaned in.

"You're not even the main objective. You're just bait."

The guy cracked. Not completely. Not obviously. But Tanner saw it.

The instructor called time, nodding slightly.

Tanner had won. But at what cost? His head was pounding, his body running on nothing but adrenaline and sheer stubbornness.

\*\*\*

By the time classes ended, Tanner felt like he'd been through a war.

His brain was fried. His body was heavy.

As he walked back to the barracks, he caught sight of Drew Lemons sitting outside, flipping through notes.

Tanner slowed.

Lemons didn't even look up, just muttered, "Long day, huh?"

Tanner exhaled. "You have no idea."

Lemons smirked, finally glancing up. "Oh, I do. And it's only going to get harder, Captain America."

Tanner shook his head. Of course it was.

He stepped inside, collapsed onto his bunk, and for the first time all day —

His brain finally shut off.

# CHAPTER 7

## THE PUGIL STICK GAUNTLET

The air smelled like sweat and dust, the afternoon sun beating down mercilessly on the training field as candidates lined up along the sandpit. The sound of wooden clacks and grunts of exertion echoed as cadets battled one another with pugil sticks, their movements quick and brutal.

Tanner rolled his shoulders, gripping the thick, padded staff in both hands. The moment the instructor had announced the pugil stick gauntlet, Tanner knew it was going to be a bloodbath.

Twelve candidates. Single elimination.

Tanner eyed the opposite end of the pit, where Drew Lemons stood, rolling his neck like a fighter preparing for a title match.

Tanner exhaled sharply.

Of course he's here.

Lemons caught his gaze and smirked.

Tanner just nodded. One fight at a time.

\*\*\*

Tanner's first opponent was a stocky, broad-shouldered cadet with a wrestler's stance. The moment the whistle blew, the guy came in low and aggressive, trying to bull-rush Tanner backward.

Tanner sidestepped, bringing the pugil stick up in a smooth, defensive block before slamming the padded tip into his opponent's ribs.

The cadet grunted but kept pushing forward, trying to grapple.

Tanner twisted, using his opponent's momentum against him, and swung hard into the side of his helmet.

The blow sent the cadet stumbling sideways, struggling to regain balance.

Tanner didn't hesitate. One final strike—straight to the chest.

The instructor blew the whistle.

"Winner—Tanner!"

Tanner stepped back, heart steady but surging with adrenaline.

One down.

\*\*\*

Tanner barely had time to catch his breath before Lemons stepped into the pit for his own match.

His opponent—a tall, wiry cadet with quick reflexes—tried to keep his distance, using speed to avoid Lemons' strikes.

For a moment, it almost looked like Lemons was losing ground.

Then—without warning—Lemons feinted left, baiting his opponent into lunging forward.

Big mistake.

Lemons pivoted hard, swinging the pugil stick in a brutal arc, smashing his opponent straight in the side of the helmet.

The cadet crashed to the ground, stunned.

The whistle blew.

"Winner—Lemons!"

Lemons rolled his shoulders, grinning, and looked straight at Tanner.

Tanner didn't react.

But he knew.

It was inevitable.

They were on a collision course.

\*\*\*

Each fight was a grueling test of endurance.

Tanner's second opponent was faster, more technical, forcing him to rely on precision strikes instead of brute force.

Lemons' next opponent was a tank, someone who took every hit and kept charging forward—but Lemons fought smarter, not harder, wearing the guy down with quick, brutal jabs before knocking him flat.

One by one, the field narrowed.

Until there were only two fighters left standing.

Chris Tanner.

Drew Lemons.

Final round.

*\*\**

The crowd around the pit had grown. Candidates leaned in, some whispering bets, others just eager to see the inevitable showdown.

Tanner and Lemons stepped into the sand, eyes locked.

The instructor's voice cut through the tension.

"Final match. No time limit. You fight until I call it."

Tanner rolled his wrists, adjusting his grip.

Lemons just smirked.

The whistle screeched.

Lemons struck first—fast and aggressive, going straight for Tanner's head.

Tanner dodged, deflecting the blow and countering with a sharp jab to Lemons' ribs.

Lemons grunted but didn't back down.

Instead, he came in low, swinging for Tanner's legs.

Tanner jumped back, barely avoiding the hit. He twisted, bringing his own pugil stick down toward Lemons' shoulder—

Blocked.

Lemons absorbed the hit, then used his momentum to slam Tanner across the chest, sending him staggering back.

Tanner barely caught himself before hitting the ground.

Lemons grinned. "You getting tired, Captain America?"

Tanner forced a breath through his nose.

"Keep talking."

Lemons lunged again.

Tanner met him head-on.

The next few exchanges were fast, brutal, and relentless—blows colliding mid-air, neither giving ground.

Then—Lemons feinted left, pivoted hard, and swung for Tanner's exposed side.

Tanner saw it.

And countered.

Both of them struck at the same time.

Tanner's pugil stick crashed into Lemons' ribs just as Lemons' slammed into Tanner's shoulder.

They both stumbled back, gasping for breath.

Neither went down.

The crowd was dead silent.

Then the instructor stepped forward.

"Enough."

Tanner blinked.

Lemons wiped the sweat from his brow, breathing hard.

The instructor looked between them.

"Final match ends in a draw."

Tanner exhaled slowly.

A draw.

He glanced at Lemons.

Lemons smirked, but this time it wasn't cocky—it was something else.

A look that said, "Alright. You're legit."

Tanner just nodded.

For the first time since arriving at OCS, they weren't just rivals.

They were equals.

And maybe, just maybe—that was worse.

# CHAPTER 8

## CAPTURE THE FLAG

The dirt beneath his fingers felt dry and loose as Tanner crouched with the rest of his squad. The squad leader sketched a rough outline of the playing field, using jagged lines to indicate obstacles and key structures.

"Alright, here's the plan," the squad leader said, his voice a harsh whisper. "We need four to stay and defend our base. Two in this building, one in the building across. The rest of us will move along the side of the bus and hit them where it hurts. The guys in the buildings— provide cover fire. If you have a shot, take it."

Tanner scanned the area, mentally mapping out his best vantage point. He tapped the shoulder of the cadet beside him. "We'll take up positions in this building," he said.

The squad leader nodded. "Good. Get to it."

Tanner and his assigned teammate broke off, moving low toward the designated building. The air was tense—this was a test, and nobody wanted to fail.

They reached the roof just in time to see the rest of their team advancing toward the bus.

Then—gunfire erupted.

Bright red marker rounds zipped through the air, striking cadets as they yelped and dropped to the ground, "eliminated" from the match.

Tanner's heart dropped.

Ambush.

The enemy had hidden inside the bus, waiting for them.

The squad leader went down instantly, along with three others.

Two survivors managed to break away, diving behind a wrecked car for cover. Tanner adjusted his rifle, shifting for a better angle on the bus.

One breath.

Two.

Fire.

His first shot clipped an enemy's shoulder. They jerked back, eliminated.

Another enemy popped up from the bus window— Tanner tagged them square in the chest.

He worked methodically, picking off each enemy as they revealed themselves.

When the last one went down, Tanner yelled to the stranded teammates: "Move! Get to cover behind this building! We'll provide cover fire!"

The two cadets hesitated before darting across the open ground.

Then—Tanner saw him.

Drew Lemons.

His jaw clenched instinctively.

Tanner swallowed his frustration and forced the words out: "Lemons! Get up here. We'll regroup and push forward."

Lemons grinned, but it wasn't one of gratitude. It was mocking, like he'd expected Tanner to be the one calling for his help instead.

Tanner ignored it. This wasn't about personal feelings.

For now.

***

Breathless, Lemons and the other cadet reached the rooftop.

"Thanks for the save," the other cadet panted.

Tanner nodded, glancing at the guy. "What's your name?"

"Bob. Bob Smith."

Tanner blinked. "No way. Your real name?"

Smith straight-faced him. "No."

A snort came from Lemons. "Shit, dude. Can you get any more generic?"

Smith didn't blink. "No."

Lemons laughed, but Tanner had no time for games. "Focus up. We need to push forward."

Lemons immediately cut in, that same cocky smirk on his face.

"I saw an exit leading to the back. Less exposure, more cover. We can use some barrels to stay hidden until we're close to their base."

Tanner's gut twisted.

That wasn't his plan.

And he hated that Lemons always had to take control.

But...it was a good route.

Tanner nodded reluctantly. "Fine. But stay sharp. No screw-ups."

Lemons' grin widened, like Tanner had just handed him something valuable.

"Lead the way, Captain America."

***

The team moved through the narrow back alley, keeping low behind stacked barrels. Tanner took point, peering around the corner.

Enemy spotted.

Tanner swung out and fired—direct hit.

They moved forward in single file, sweeping toward the base. Tanner was hyper-focused on the entrance, reading for the next enemy to pop out.

Then—a body slammed into his back.

Tanner stumbled, nearly losing his footing.

"What the hell?!" he snapped.

Lemons had pushed past him, moving aggressively toward the base.

Tanner's stomach burned with frustration.

You just had to be the first one in, didn't you, Lemons?

Gunfire erupted again.

Tanner and Lemons both reacted, taking out two more enemies before they could fire back.

Smith wasn't so lucky. He took a round to the chest, his vest flashing bright red.

"Shit! I'm out!" Smith groaned.

Lemons barely acknowledged him. He was already scanning the enemy base, planning his next move.

"There's a boarded-up window on the left," Lemons said. "I'll pop smoke on the right and draw their fire. You breach the window and grab the flag."

Tanner hesitated.

This felt too easy.

"What if there are more inside?" Tanner asked.

Lemons rolled his eyes. "Dude, just follow the plan. Unless you're scared?"

Tanner's jaw tensed.

He had two choices.

1. Trust Lemons and push forward.

2. Ignore him and risk losing momentum.

Tanner cursed under his breath.

"Fine," he muttered.

He moved toward the boarded-up window, keeping low. Lemons signaled, then tossed the smoke grenade.

A thick cloud of gray mist erupted on the opposite side of the base.

The enemy took the bait.

Gunfire ripped through the smoke, directed toward the wrong side.

Tanner didn't waste a second.

He sprinted, leaped, and crashed through the window, rolling inside.

Before the enemy could react, his hands were on the flag.

***

The air horn blasted.

Game over.

Tanner barely had time to process before Smith and another cadet rushed past him—straight to Lemons.

"Good job, Lemons! That was a solid plan!"

Pat on the back.

Another.

Lemons basked in it, grinning ear to ear like he was the one who had grabbed the damn flag.

Tanner stood off to the side, his elation fading into irritation.

He'd done the work.

Lemons had just played the game better.

Tanner clenched his fists, swallowing down the bitter taste of second place.

This wasn't over.

# CHAPTER 9

## CQB TRAINING

The air inside the shoot house was thick with the smell of gun oil and sweat. Overhead, the fluorescent lights flickered, casting harsh shadows over the reinforced plywood walls.

Tanner adjusted his grip on the M4 training rifle, the weight familiar but heavier today.

This wasn't just another drill.

This was Close Quarters Battle (CQB) training—a test of speed, accuracy, and decision-making in high-stress environments.

And today, it was a competition.

Tanner exhaled, rolling his shoulders.

Across the prep area, Drew Lemons leaned casually against a crate, tapping his helmet with a smug grin.

"Hope you didn't skip breakfast, Captain America. Wouldn't want you getting lightheaded when you see my score."

Tanner smirked. "You should be more worried about yours."

Lemons chuckled. "Oh, I'm not. I plan on setting the bar so high, you'll need a damn ladder to reach it."

Tanner said nothing.

He was done talking.

It was time to prove it.

***

The instructor, a grizzled Master Sergeant with a scar running down his forearm, stood before the class, arms crossed.

"This is as close to real combat as it gets in a controlled environment. You'll be graded on:

- Time to clear the course
- Accuracy on enemy targets
- Proper handling of civilians and hostages
- Overall tactical movement

"One bad call, one hesitation, one friendly fire mistake—" he gestured toward a list of disqualified cadets from previous runs, "—and you're done."

Tanner tightened his grip on his rifle.

The shoot house was a complex maze of narrow hallways, blind corners, and staged rooms, each one holding either an enemy combatant, a civilian, or a high-value target.

No one knew the exact layout until they breached the door.

Tanner scanned the order list.

Lemons' name was just before his.

Perfect.

He'd know exactly what time he had to beat.

*** 

The air crackled with tension as Lemons stepped up to the start line, slipping his helmet into place.

"Shooter ready?" the instructor called.

Lemons nodded, his smirk never fading.

"Go!"

The metal door slammed open, and Lemons was gone—a blur of motion as he entered the first room.

Tanner stood near the monitor, watching the live feed from the overhead cameras.

Lemons moved like he'd done this a hundred times before—fluid, aggressive, every step calculated.

POP-POP-POP!

His rifle snapped up three quick headshots, dropping enemy targets with precision.

A civilian appeared—Lemons angled his weapon away, clearing the next corner.

Another target—double-tap center mass.

He was fast.

Tanner felt his fingers twitching.

Then—the hostage scenario.

Lemons cleared the room, raising his weapon—but the hostage was in the line of fire.

Tanner leaned in.

Does he take the shot?

Lemons hesitated—just for a fraction of a second.

Then—he adjusted his angle and fired.

Headshot.

"Time!"

The scoreboard flashed.

1 minute, 32.6 seconds.

Lemons stepped out of the course, pulling off his helmet, his grin practically splitting his face.

He looked straight at Tanner.

"Try to keep up."

Tanner rolled his neck, stepping up to the line.

"Shooter ready?"

He exhaled.

"Ready."

"Go!"

\*\*\*

The door slammed open, and Tanner exploded forward.

First room—three targets.

He fired in a controlled burst.

POP-POP-POP.

All three went down.

No wasted movement.

Tanner ducked into the hallway, pivoting left—an enemy came out from cover.

Squeeze. Fire. Drop.

The next room. Civilian in the open.

Tanner angled his rifle away, scanning for threats before moving forward.

The hall narrowed. He heard movement ahead.

Think.

Tanner dropped low, sweeping the corner fast—

Hostile!

He fired a single shot, dropping the target before moving on.

The final room loomed ahead.

The hostage scenario.

Tanner's heart slammed in his chest.

He burst through the doorway—enemy behind a hostage.

He could hear Lemons' voice in his head.

"Hesitate, and you lose."

Tanner didn't hesitate.

He angled his rifle just right—one inch off from center.

Squeeze. Fire.

The shot whizzed past the hostage's ear, hitting the hostile dead center.

"Time!"

Tanner lowered his rifle, sucking in deep breaths as the instructor checked the stopwatch.

"1 minute… 31.8 seconds."

Tanner's jaw tightened.

He had beaten Lemons' time.

By less than a second.

*\*\*\**

Tanner stepped out of the course, pulling off his helmet, his hair damp with sweat.

The air was thick with tension, the kind that comes when something shifts and one person isn't ready for it.

Lemons stood there, arms crossed, jaw tight.

His smirk? Gone.

His usual easy arrogance? Nowhere to be found.

Instead, there was something harder, colder, simmering just beneath the surface.

Tanner locked eyes with him.

"You were saying?"

Lemons scoffed, but it wasn't his usual carefree, smug response.

It was forced. Tense.

"Bullshit."

Tanner arched an eyebrow. "What's that? Didn't catch it over the sound of your time flashing behind mine."

Lemons' nostrils flared.

"You got lucky." His voice was sharp, clipped, nothing like his usual easy-going taunts. "Next time, you won't."

Tanner smirked, but there was no gloating behind it—just quiet satisfaction.

"Guess we'll find out."

Lemons shook his head, yanking off his gloves and slamming them onto the equipment bench. His movements were too aggressive, a barely-contained storm.

Tanner had seen Lemons mad before.

But this was different. This wasn't irritation. This was Lemons realizing, maybe for the first time, that he wasn't the best anymore. And he hated it.

Tanner turned away, heading toward the rest of the cadets who had been watching. He had nothing else to prove.

But as he walked off, he could still feel Lemons' glare burning into his back.

# CHAPTER 10

## THE SAND TABLE BRIEFING

The fluorescent lights buzzed overhead as Tanner walked into the room, the faint scent of coffee and sweat lingering in the air. The walls were lined with maps, strategic diagrams, and training schedules, but the focal point was in the center—a large, rectangular sand table filled with miniature buildings, terrain models, and carefully placed markers representing units.

This wasn't just another test.

This was leadership on display.

Tanner swallowed hard as he stepped into line with the other candidates. His shoulders stiffened when he spotted Captain Scott standing near the back, arms crossed, expression unreadable.

She was watching.

And that meant failure wasn't an option.

The instructor, a grizzled Master Sergeant, stood at the front, tapping a pointer stick against the edge of the table.

"This is a simple mission. Your objective is to infiltrate, neutralize enemy positions, and secure this structure here—" he pointed at a three-story building in the center of the table, "—before reinforcements arrive."

His eyes swept over them.

"Each of you will take turns briefing your plan. You'll have five minutes to develop a strategy. Then, you'll present it to the group. Questions?"

No one spoke.

"Good. Tanner, you're up first."

Tanner's stomach dropped.

First? Shit.

***

Tanner stepped forward, eyes scanning the sand table, his mind racing.

Five minutes to plan. No hesitation. Think.

He traced the map with his finger. The objective was clear—breach and secure the target building. But the enemy controlled the two outer structures, which meant any direct approach would be a kill zone.

He exhaled sharply and started speaking.

"We'll split into two assault teams. One will lay down suppressing fire while the other flanks from the right. We'll use smoke to cover movement, breach the southern entrance, and clear room by room."

He paused.

The room was dead silent.

The Master Sergeant's expression didn't change.

Tanner licked his lips. Did I miss something?

He glanced around the table again, then added, "Once the structure is secure, we'll reposition to hold against reinforcements."

Another pause.

"That's it?" the Master Sergeant asked.

Tanner hesitated. "Sir?"

The instructor's lips twitched.

"You just got your whole squad killed, Tanner."

Tanner's blood ran cold.

\*\*\*

The Master Sergeant snatched up a stick and gestured at the board, sharp and deliberate.

"You split your forces in two, but didn't account for the enemy sniper position here—" he jabbed at a rooftop marker, "—which means the moment your flank team moves in, they get lit up. Your fire support gets suppressed, your breach team is isolated, and now you're stuck in a building you don't control, boxed in with enemy reinforcements on the way.**"

Tanner's throat went dry.

The Master Sergeant leaned in. "Now, let me ask you this. What do you do?"

Tanner's brain stalled.

Think. Think.

The other candidates watched him, waiting.

He took a breath, forcing his panic down.

"Sir, I would—"

"Too late. You're dead."

Tanner's jaw clenched.

The Master Sergeant tossed the pointer onto the sand table. "Tanner, let me make this clear—hesitation will kill you faster than bullets. You don't get to second-guess yourself in command. You make a call, and you live with the consequences. Or your people don't live at all."

Tanner nodded stiffly.

"Reset the table. Let's try this again."

***

Tanner studied the sand table again.

This time, something was different.

The sniper's position had been moved. No longer sitting on an obvious rooftop, it was now marked within an upper-story window, giving him partial visibility of the main approach but a narrower field of fire.

It was a more concealed but still dangerous location—an adjustment to test him.

Tanner adjusted his plan.

"We'll start with a two-man fire team positioned here, overlooking the suspected sniper's hide. The sniper will be the first target—we take them out immediately before the main assault moves in."

He pointed to the ridge behind the objective.

"We insert a sniper of our own, positioned here. Once our sniper is set, we initiate a brief feint attack from the east, baiting the enemy's attention. The moment they react, our sniper neutralizes the threat in the window, eliminating the overwatch."

Tanner gained confidence, moving his hands across the map.

"With their sniper gone, we move forward in a coordinated push—fire support suppresses the building while the breach team closes the distance. We use smoke for concealment and enter from two points."

Tanner looked around the sand table, noting a taller building adjacent to the target structure.

He tapped it.

"Instead of fast-roping, the second team gains rooftop access from this adjacent building. They move across, securing high ground before engaging any remaining rooftop threats."

The Master Sergeant raised an eyebrow.

"You're banking on that rooftop move working. What if you get pinned?"

Tanner responded without hesitation.

"If the rooftop team gets pinned, we have fire support suppressing enemy positions. The breach team will push hard from the ground level to force the defenders to split their focus. The moment they do, the rooftop team seizes their opening and completes the breach from above."

The Master Sergeant's expression stayed unreadable, but he gave a small nod.

"Better," he said.

Tanner let out a slow breath.

Not perfect. But better.

***

As Tanner stepped back, he felt a weight on him—a gaze.

His eyes flickered toward Captain Scott.

She was still watching, arms crossed, expression neutral—but there was something in her eyes.

Approval? Amusement? He couldn't tell.

But she hadn't dismissed him. And that was enough.

For now.

# CHAPTER 11

## LAND NAVIGATION

The wind rustled through the dense treetops as Tanner stood at the edge of the tree line, arms crossed, listening to the instructor lay out the conditions of the mission.

"You will pair up in groups of two or three. Use your maps and compass to navigate to the LZ for extraction at twenty-three hundred hours." The instructor's eyes scanned over the cadets before delivering the kicker. "If you miss the chopper, it's a ten-mile hike back to the barracks. And if you screw up?" He smirked. "Hope you enjoy a cold, wet night, because there's a storm rolling in late tonight."

Tanner barely had to think about his partner. He already knew who he wanted to keep an eye on.

He turned to Drew Lemons.

"Lemons, you and me. Let's go."

Lemons arched an eyebrow, the usual smug glint in his eyes. He didn't even argue—just snatched up a compass, shoved it into his pocket, and followed Tanner into the woods.

Tanner tightened his grip on his map. He wasn't about to let Lemons pull any shit tonight.

\*\*\*

Hours passed as they hiked deep into the forest, the sun dropping lower behind the tree line.

Tanner squinted at his map, tracing his finger along a ridgeline they'd been following. He glanced at the compass and nodded. "Lemons, this is freakin' easy. We're making great time. If we keep this pace, we'll reach the LZ in a couple of hours."

Lemons huffed, taking a long swig from his canteen. "Yeah, but look at this." He jabbed at the map. "We've been following this ridge. If we slide down the side, cut through this valley, we can shave off at least an hour."

Tanner frowned. "I don't know—"

"Come on, Captain America." Lemons grinned, taunting. "What's the worst that could happen?"

Tanner exhaled through his nose, forcing himself to ignore the insult. He glanced at the darkening sky.

Saving an hour could mean getting out before the storm hit.

"...Fine," he muttered. "Let's do it."

They adjusted course, descending the steep ridge and into the valley below. The moment they set foot at the bottom, the sun disappeared completely behind the ridge.

Darkness set in fast.

\*\*\*

Time stretched, and so did the terrain. The valley was deceptively long, and the incline on the other side was steeper than expected.

Tanner wiped the sweat from his forehead and exhaled. "Lemons, hold up. Let me see the compass so we can check our bearing."

Lemons froze.

Tanner watched as Lemons patted his pockets, his face twisting into something between confusion and forced panic.

"Shit. I can't find the compass."

Tanner stopped walking. Stared.

"...Ha. Ha. Very funny. Quit screwing around."

"I'm serious, man." Lemons widened his eyes, putting on a convincing look of concern. "I must've dropped it when we came down the ridge."

Tanner's gut twisted. Something felt off.

Lemons was a lot of things—reckless, arrogant, a pain in the ass—but careless? No way.

"You've gotta be kidding me." Tanner's voice was dangerously low.

Lemons shrugged. "Look, we'll just keep heading up. Maybe we can see better from higher ground."

Tanner clenched his jaw. No choice. He'd deal with this later.

"Fine," he muttered. "Let's go."

\*\*\*

After twenty more minutes of trudging uphill, Tanner stopped.

"This is pointless. We need to confirm our direction before we waste more time."

Lemons threw his arms out. "And how exactly do you plan to do that, Einstein?"

Tanner ignored him, glancing at the clear sky overhead.

"I heard once that if you line up the top of two trees with a star, the direction the star moves in will tell you which way you're facing."

Lemons let out a snort. "Oh, yeah? And did your grandpappy tell you that before tucking you in? Sounds like a load of bullshit."

Tanner exhaled sharply, forcing his frustration down. "Just give me five minutes."

Lemons sighed dramatically and began tapping his foot, obnoxiously loud.

Minutes crawled by.

Lemons slapped Tanner's arm. "Dude, this will never work. The storm's rolling in, and I do NOT wanna be out here when it hits."

Tanner squinted at the star's movement. There.

"It moved down and to the right." Tanner turned to Lemons, triumphant. "Which means we're facing southwest, and we need to head north."

Lemons rolled his eyes. "Lucky guess."

Tanner didn't care. He knew they were on the right track now.

"Let's move," he ordered.

For once, Lemons didn't argue.

***

They hiked for another hour, stopping only to catch their breath and sip water.

Then—the distant whirl of helicopter blades.

Tanner's heart leapt.

"We're close!" he shouted, breaking into a sprint toward the clearing.

The trees thinned. The wind whipped against them.

Tanner burst through the tree line—just in time to see the chopper lifting off.

"FUCK!" Tanner dropped to his knees, panting, watching their ticket home disappear into the night sky.

From behind them, a car door slammed.

Tanner and Lemons turned to see the instructor standing by his truck, arms crossed, shaking his head.

"Looks like you two dipshits get to walk back to base," he said flatly.

Tanner's stomach dropped.

The truck engine revved, and within seconds, the instructor was gone, leaving them alone in the field.

The sky rumbled in the distance.

Tanner exhaled sharply. This was going to be a long, wet night.

\*\*\*

Tanner's boots squelched in the mud, the last remnants of rain soaking through his fatigues as he trudged toward the barracks. His body was aching, his legs felt like lead, and his patience was damn near gone.

They had missed the extraction chopper.

They had walked miles in the dark, drenched, exhausted, and forced to rely on the stars to navigate their way back to base.

And it was all because of one thing.

The missing compass.

Tanner had let it slide when Lemons had claimed he lost it, chalking it up to bad luck, exhaustion, or carelessness.

But something felt off.

And as they stepped onto the barracks porch, Tanner caught something shiny slipping from under Lemons' blouse.

A cord. A compass.

Tanner snatched it before Lemons could react, yanking it free and holding it up in the dim light.

His stomach turned.

"You son of a—" Tanner's voice was low, lethal.

Lemons didn't flinch. Didn't even try to deny it. Instead, his lips curled into a smirk.

Tanner's grip tightened around the compass.

"You had it the whole time."

Lemons tilted his head, as if considering his answer. Then, with zero shame, he shrugged.

"Looks that way, doesn't it?"

Tanner's blood boiled.

"You did this on purpose." His voice was dangerously steady, the anger boiling just beneath the surface.

Lemons' smirk widened. "You think?"

Tanner took a step closer, chest to chest, the exhaustion of the night making his temper razor thin.

"Why?"

Lemons let out a slow breath, shaking his head.

Then, in the same mocking, smug tone that had gotten under Tanner's skin since day one, he said:

"Consider it payback."

Tanner stared, fury laced through every inch of his body.

Lemons leaned in slightly, voice dropping just enough so no one else could hear.

"You embarrassed me in CQB. Took my win. My time." His smirk faltered, just slightly. "So I figured, why not take something from you?"

Tanner felt his jaw clench so hard it ached.

This wasn't just a rivalry anymore.

Lemons had sabotaged him.

Made them miss the chopper. Forced them to march through the night.

Put them both in a position where things could have gone seriously wrong.

And all because he lost?

Tanner took a slow breath, forcing himself to step back.

Punching Lemons wouldn't do anything but land them both in deep shit.

But one thing was clear.

This wasn't over.

Not by a long shot.

Tanner tossed the compass at Lemons' chest, hard enough that Lemons had to catch it.

"Enjoy the win, Lemons."

Lemons' smirk returned. "Oh, I will."

Tanner turned away, shoving open the barracks door.

But as he walked inside, shaking with barely-contained fury, he made himself a silent promise.

Next time, Lemons wouldn't get the chance to screw him over.

Next time, he would be ready.

# CHAPTER 12

## THE STRESS INTERVIEW

The room was small, windowless, and suffocatingly sterile. A single metal chair sat in the center, directly under a blinding overhead light. The walls were bare, the air stale, and the silence unsettling. On one side of the room, a large, darkened panel of glass reflected the harsh light back at him. Tanner's gut told him it wasn't just a window—it was a one-way mirror. Tanner knew someone was watching.

Possibly Captain Scott.

Tanner stood at attention just inside the door, back straight, fists clenched at his sides. His uniform, still damp from the miserable hike back from land navigation, clung to his skin, making him itch with discomfort.

Across from him sat a panel of officers, their expressions unreadable. A Colonel, a Major, and a man in civilian clothes—but he carried himself like someone used to being in charge.

Tanner didn't know his name. He didn't like that.

"Candidate Tanner," the Colonel finally spoke, flipping through a thick file on the table.

Tanner held his stance. "Sir."

The Colonel hummed. "At ease. Sit down."

Tanner obeyed, lowering himself onto the chair. The second his ass hit the metal, the interrogation began.

***

The Colonel didn't look up from the file.

"Chris Tanner. Born and raised in St. Louis. No siblings. Father left when you were nine."

Tanner kept his expression neutral.

"Your mother—deeply religious. Seems like she spent more time at church than at home. Is that why you joined? Needed structure?"

Tanner kept his face still. "No, sir."

"Why then?"

"I wanted to serve."

The Colonel flipped a page.

"Or did you just want to escape?"

Tanner's fingers tightened against his knee.

"Sir, I joined because I believe in something bigger than myself."

The Colonel glanced up, finally meeting his eyes.

"And what exactly is that, Tanner?"

Tanner swallowed.

What the hell kind of question was that?

"...Serving my country, sir."

The Colonel let the silence stretch, watching him.

Tanner kept his face neutral, but something about the way the officers exchanged glances put him on edge.

They were waiting for something.

***

The Major took over.

"Tell me about the theater."

Tanner's body went rigid. No.

"Sir?"

The Major's eyes were too knowing.

"The day you changed your departure date. You saw your best friend with your girlfriend. You lost your temper." He tapped the file. "Seems like an impulsive decision to uproot your entire life."

Tanner's stomach clenched.

He hadn't thought about that day since he arrived at OCS.

He forced his jaw not to tighten. "With respect, sir, my reasons for enlisting are not based on personal matters."

"Aren't they?"

Tanner's fingers dug into his pants leg.

The Major leaned forward. "You threw a punch in the middle of a crowded shopping mall. That's a loss of control."

Tanner felt his pulse pound in his ears.

"You don't lose control in combat." The Major's voice was low, sharp. "Because if you do, people die."

Tanner took a measured breath, forcing himself to focus.

This was a test.

He met the Major's stare head-on. "I am fully capable of controlling my emotions, sir."

The Major's eyes flickered. For a moment, Tanner swore he saw the hint of a smirk.

Like he'd just given them exactly what they wanted.

\*\*\*

The civilian finally spoke. His voice was smooth, calm—too calm.

"Tell me, Candidate Tanner. If someone under your command betrayed you, what would you do?"

Tanner's breath hitched for just a second.

He didn't answer right away.

The civilian watched him closely.

Tanner exhaled through his nose. "Depends on the circumstances, sir."

"Fair enough," the man nodded. "Would you still trust them? Work beside them?"

Tanner's jaw flexed.

"...Trust would be difficult to rebuild."

"So, no."

Tanner hesitated. He didn't like the way this was going.

"Would you trust yourself in that situation?" the man pressed.

Tanner blinked.

"Sir?"

"If you made the wrong call—if your actions cost lives—would you still trust yourself?"

The question hit him like a gut punch. His throat felt tight. This isn't a normal interview. Something about this felt off.

He straightened his spine, pushing the discomfort down. "If I made the wrong call, sir, I would own it. Learn from it. Make sure it never happened again."

The man smiled slightly. "Good answer."

Tanner wasn't sure if he'd actually passed that question or not.

As he slid a satellite image across the table to Tanner, The Major spoke, voice sharp and clinical.

"You are leading a recovery operation. An unmanned drone carrying classified data was downed behind enemy lines. Your mission: locate the wreckage, extract the black box, and return to base before enemy forces arrive. You have a four-man team, limited supplies, and no air support."

Tanner's mind clicked into gear. Straightforward. Infiltrate, recover, exfil.

"I'd take the northern approach, using the tree line for concealment. Move under cover of night, retrieve the black box, and exfil along the riverbed to avoid foot patrols."

The Major nodded slightly.

"Good."

Sliding another image across a thermal image of a second crash site.

"New development. Another aircraft has gone down—this time, a manned one."

Tanner felt his pulse tick up slightly.

The Major continued.

"One survivor. A high-value VIP. Injured. Unable to move without assistance. Enemy forces are closing in. You still need to recover the black box, but now you must also extract the VIP."

Tanner barely blinked.

"Adjusting priorities. The VIP is now primary. We move to their location first. Two men secure the perimeter while one administers aid. If their condition is critical, we call for emergency evac. If not, we move on foot to exfil."

The Major's brow arched slightly.

"And the black box? It was the original mission. Are you willing to abandon it?"

Tanner didn't hesitate.

"No, sir. We'll secure the VIP first, stabilize them, and reposition to retrieve the black box after assessing the threat level. If the area is too hot, we prioritize the VIP and leave the box behind. It's important, but a life comes first."

The psych officer made a quick note. The Major's expression stayed unreadable.

"You had ten minutes. That answer took thirty seconds. Are you sure?"

Tanner's jaw tightened.

"Yes, sir. If I overthink in the field, people die."

The Major sat back, studying him.

Then he nodded.

\*\*\*

The Colonel closed the file. "Last question."

Tanner braced himself.

"Would you rather save five soldiers and fail the mission… or complete the mission, knowing those five would die?"

Tanner felt a weight settle on his chest. This was it. The question that defined leadership. There was no right answer. Only a choice.

Tanner thought about it. Really thought about it.

And he realized… There was only one thing he could say.

"Sir, I'd find a way to do both."

Silence. Then, the Colonel's smirk returned.

"That's what they all say."

Tanner's stomach dropped.

The Colonel stood. "You're dismissed."

Tanner stood, saluted, and walked out the door, his mind spinning.

***

From behind a one-way mirror, Captain Alison Scott watched him leave.

The Colonel turned to her, arching an eyebrow. "Well?"

Scott tapped a finger against her chin, thoughtful.

"He's got the right instincts."

The Colonel nodded. "He hesitated, but he answered the way he should have. Still needs pressure-testing."

Scott smirked. "Oh, don't worry. I'll make sure he gets plenty of that."

The Colonel chuckled. "Poor bastard has no idea what he's in for."

# CHAPTER 13

## THE BARRACKS NIGHT RAID

Tanner was dreaming of home—but it was one of those dreams where everything felt just a little off. The front door was open. His mom's voice was calling, but the words didn't make sense.

Then—BOOM.

The door to the barracks slammed open, a deafening flashbang of sound.

Shouts erupted in the hall.

"MOVE! MOVE! MOVE!"

The piercing wail of alarms drowned out the groggy confusion as the entire barracks exploded into chaos.

Tanner jolted upright, his brain still lagging behind reality.

What the—

A raid.

His body snapped into action before his mind could catch up.

***

The overhead lights stayed dark, replaced by the eerie strobe of red emergency lights flickering down the hall.

Tanner threw off his blanket, heart hammering. He could barely make out figures moving—some still tangled in sheets, others scrambling for their gear.

Then the air rattled with gunfire—simulated blanks, but they sounded real enough in the moment.

Tanner grabbed his training rifle, still propped against his bunk from earlier. He was ready.

Others weren't.

Cadets tripped over each other, scrambling for gear, some still trying to process what was happening.

This is a test.

Tanner's mind clicked into place as he watched Lemons shove past a cadet, making a beeline for the exit.

Of course, he was.

Lemons was racing to take control before anyone else.

Not tonight.

Tanner made his move.

"SQUAD, FORM UP!"

Tanner's voice cut through the noise like a knife.

Some cadets hesitated—but they gravitated toward him, desperate for any kind of direction.

"Get your weapons, check your gear—" he motioned to the door, "—we need to secure the hall! Whoever's already armed, on me! MOVE!"

No one else had taken control.

So they listened.

Tanner grabbed the nearest cadet—Smith, the guy with the generic name.

"Smith, take three guys and cover the back entrance. If this is an assault, we need to stop them from boxing us in."

Smith nodded and took off.

Tanner turned just as Lemons pushed his way forward.

"The hell are you doing, Tanner?" Lemons demanded, stepping into his space.

Tanner didn't flinch. "Making sure we don't get steamrolled. Got a problem?"

Lemons' eyes flashed like he was about to argue—

But then gunfire cracked again, closer this time.

No time.

"Fine, whatever. But if you screw this up—"

Tanner was already moving.

***

Tanner pressed against the doorframe, rifle raised as he peeked into the hall.

Figures in full tactical gear were moving methodically, sweeping the corridor, their rifles trained on the doorways.

The instructors.

A voice boomed from down the hall.

"CLEAR ROOM TO ROOM! MOVE!"

Tanner's pulse spiked.

They were coming straight for them.

"LEMONS! Cover the left side! Smith, status?!"

"Rear secure! No movement!"

Tanner took a breath. They had one chance to hold this position.

"We set up here, make them fight for it. We delay, they don't clear this hallway easily. Hold the line!"

***

The first breach team reached their position.

Tanner squeezed the trigger—his rifle snapped with simulated fire, and the lead instructor went down with a flash of red.

"Contact front!"

The cadets poured fire down the hall, knocking out two more instructors before they adjusted tactics.

The counterattack came fast.

A simulated flashbang bounced into the room—

Tanner reacted first.

"FLASH! GET DOWN!"

He dove behind a bunk, yanking Smith with him just as the training grenade detonated.

Bright white light flooded the space, but they were out of the blast radius.

Tanner didn't waste a second. He popped up and fired, taking down another enemy.

That was when he saw it.

Lemons was hesitating.

Tanner spotted him ducked behind cover, rifle tight in his grip—but he wasn't firing.

Tanner's stomach clenched.

Lemons was calculating. Waiting.

Letting Tanner take the risk.

Tanner made a split-second decision.

"Lemons, MOVE!" he barked.

Lemons snapped to attention, then—maybe out of instinct, maybe out of pressure—he finally moved into action.

Tanner and Lemons pushed forward together, taking down the last two instructors in their zone.

The hall fell silent.

And then—

"END EXERCISE!"

A loud air horn blasted through the barracks, signaling the end of the raid.

Tanner's chest rose and fell with heavy breaths.

That was it. They had held.

And Lemons?

Lemons had followed Tanner's order.

\*\*\*

Tanner stood with his team, waiting for the instructors to finish their evaluation.

The lead instructor paced in front of them, arms crossed.

Finally, he nodded toward Tanner.

"Tanner, solid work. You saw the situation and took control. Held your ground."

Tanner kept his expression neutral, but inside, something stirred.

Then the instructor's gaze slid to Lemons.

"Lemons. Your first move was running for the exit. Not a great look."

Tanner saw Lemons' jaw tighten. He didn't argue. Didn't smirk. For the first time, Lemons had nothing to say.

And that's when Tanner knew.

This time, he'd won.

# CHAPTER 14

## MAJOR OUTDOOR COMBAT EXERCISE

The roar of helicopter blades tore through the sky as Tanner crouched low behind a fallen tree, his rifle tight against his chest. The cool night air was thick with tension, every breath filled with the distant crackle of simulated gunfire.

Somewhere beyond the ridgeline, an enemy team was waiting — other cadets, just like him, ready to prove themselves in the largest field exercise yet.

This wasn't a drill in the barracks.

This was war.

And Chris Tanner was in command.

\*\*\*

Earlier that evening, the candidates had been divided into two teams—Alpha Team (Tanner's squad) and Bravo Team (opposing force). Their objective was simple:

Secure the enemy base, eliminate resistance, and hold until sunrise.

The challenge? A 20-square-mile area of rugged, wooded terrain.

Limited ammo. No comms. Full tactical autonomy.

This was their first true leadership test.

Tanner stood at the center of his team, studying the tactical map spread across a log. The glow from a red-lensed flashlight illuminated the terrain features.

"We have two hours to reach the objective," Tanner whispered. "Bravo Team is already ahead of us. They know we're coming."

Around him, his squad of twelve cadets nodded, faces half-hidden in the shadows.

Lemons sat near the edge of the group, his expression unreadable.

Tanner could feel his presence like a thorn in his side.

But unlike before, Lemons wasn't leading this time. Tanner was.

And that meant Lemons had to follow.

Tanner traced a path on the map.

"Bravo Team will expect us to attack directly from the south. That's the fastest route, but it's also the most obvious. If we walk into an ambush, we'll be cut down before we get close."

Some of the cadets shifted uncomfortably.

"Instead, we're moving east, through the ravine. It's rough terrain, but it gives us cover. Once we reach this ridge, we'll split into two teams."

Tanner pointed at the map.

"Team One will make noise here, drawing their attention. Team Two—" He looked at Lemons, locking eyes. "—will flank from the west and breach their perimeter."

Lemons smirked. "Giving me the fun part, huh?"

Tanner kept his voice steady. "Just don't screw it up."

Lemons' smirk twitched, but he said nothing.

"We hit them hard and fast. We take the base. We hold until dawn. Understood?"

A hushed chorus of "Yes, sir."

Tanner took a breath.

This was it.

"Move out."

The night swallowed them whole as they moved through the trees, the forest alive with the quiet sounds of boots crunching dirt, breath controlled, weapons held tight.

Tanner's heartbeat matched the rhythm of his steps—steady, focused.

He could barely see past the trees, only catching glimpses of dark figures moving beside him.

Every shadow felt like a potential threat.

After an hour of hiking through the ravine, they reached the ridge.

Tanner raised his fist. Halt.

The squad dropped low, disappearing into the undergrowth.

Through the trees ahead, the enemy's base came into view—a fortified cabin with two lookout positions, dimly illuminated by a single red tactical light.

Tanner lifted his binoculars.

Two sentries on patrol. No immediate sign of the others.

Perfect.

He turned to his team, whispering, "Team One, move into position. Wait for my signal."

Lemons crouched beside him, grinning.

"Hope you know what you're doing, Captain America."

Tanner ignored him. "Go."

Lemons' fire team slipped away into the darkness.

Now all Tanner could do was wait.

The night stretched long.

Then—movement.

Lemons' team was in position.

Tanner raised his rifle and fired a single shot into the trees.

The crack split the silence.

Inside the base, the sentries jerked to attention. One shouted, "CONTACT SOUTH!"

Just like that—Team One opened fire.

Tanner's squad lit up the ridge with suppressing fire, making it seem like a full-frontal assault.

From the west, Lemons' team struck.

Gunfire erupted as they breached the perimeter, taking out the sentries before they could react.

Tanner's squad pushed forward, sprinting across open ground.

A burst of gunfire snapped past Tanner's shoulder.

He hit the dirt, rolling behind a fallen tree as Bravo Team returned fire.

"PUSH FORWARD!" he shouted.

The battle descended into chaos.

Tanner's fire team reached the base seconds before the defenders could regroup.

He kicked open the side door—Lemons was already inside, his rifle raised.

Their eyes met.

For the first time, Lemons didn't look like he was competing.

Tanner nodded.

"Clear the upstairs. I'll cover the entrance."

Lemons hesitated—just for a second—then nodded back.

And for once, he followed orders.

\*\*\*

It was just before sunrise when the final attack came.

Tanner had barely closed his eyes when a whispered warning reached his ears.

"Movement outside."

He shot upright, grabbed his rifle, and peeked through a broken window.

Figures in the trees. Lots of them.

Bravo Team was making one last push.

"Everyone up! We're under attack!"

His team scrambled to their positions—but they were almost out of ammo.

"Smith, how many rounds you got?"

"Three."

"Lemons?"

"One mag left, maybe ten shots."

Tanner gritted his teeth. They weren't going to win this with bullets.

Think, damn it.

Then—an idea.

Tanner turned to the room.

A pile of metal folding chairs, crates, and even a broken piece of plywood.

"Barricades. Now. We hold them at the entrance. Close quarters. If they breach, we take them hand-to-hand."

The squad moved fast, stacking furniture against the doors, breaking off table legs as improvised clubs.

Tanner ripped a fire extinguisher off the wall.

If they came through—he'd blind them.

Seconds stretched.

Then—the first body slammed into the door.

Bravo Team was here.

Tanner gripped his rifle tight, pulse steady.

The door shuddered—then burst open.

Bravo Team surged in.

Tanner squeezed the trigger, taking down the first attacker.

Then it was chaos.

Smith swung a chair leg, catching a cadet in the ribs.

Lemons tackled another to the ground, locking them in a grappling hold.

Tanner emptied his last shots, then grabbed the fire extinguisher, spraying white mist into the faces of the attackers.

Shouts. Confusion.

Then—an air horn blast.

"END EXERCISE!"

***

As they regrouped, the lead instructor strode into the clearing, arms crossed.

"Well." He glanced around at the exhausted, dirt-covered cadets.

"Alpha Team secured the objective. Bravo Team failed to retake it. That's a mission success."

Tanner exhaled, his chest rising with the first real breath he'd taken in hours.

"Tanner."

Tanner straightened.

"Solid leadership. You had a plan, you adapted, and you held. That's what we're looking for."

A murmur of agreement from the other instructors.

Tanner felt a flicker of something foreign.

Pride.

Then—his eyes landed on Lemons.

And for once, Lemons wasn't smirking.

He wasn't scowling, either.

Just…watching.

For the first time, Tanner had led, and Lemons had followed.

And that victory meant more than anything.

# CHAPTER 15

## HELL NIGHT

The night was cold, black, and endless. Tanner's muscles ached, his breath coming in sharp, controlled bursts as he trudged through the uneven terrain, rifle heavy in his hands. The mud sucked at his boots, each step feeling like wading through quicksand.

The only sounds were the distant rustle of trees, the occasional snap of a branch, and the labored breathing of the cadets beside him.

They were deep into Hell Night—the final, grueling test of OCS.

And it was living up to its name.

\*\*\*

The candidates had been briefed just before sundown.

This wasn't just an endurance event. It was a simulated combat operation, designed to push them past their breaking points.

- 30 miles of forced rucking through swamps, hills, and rocky terrain.
- Sleep deprivation. No rest, no stopping, no food beyond what they carried.
- Live fire stress drills, testing their accuracy and decision-making under extreme fatigue.
- Combat scenarios, where they had to make leadership calls on the fly.
- A captured VIP mission—find and extract a high-value asset from enemy territory.

It was meant to break them.

Tanner wasn't going to let it.

\*\*\*

"Tanner, you're up."

Tanner jerked his head up, blinking away exhaustion. His body screamed for rest, but he ignored it, stepping forward to take his next task.

A sharp-eyed captain stood before him, arms crossed.

"Land nav checkpoint. Your team has ten minutes to confirm your location and identify the best route to the extraction point."

Tanner kneeled, pulling out his map and compass. The glowstick hanging from his vest cast just enough light to read.

He focused.

The terrain was unfamiliar, but he worked fast, scanning for elevation changes and cross-checking distances.

Behind him, someone huffed impatiently.

"Come on, Tanner, what's taking so long?"

Tanner didn't need to look up. He knew that voice. Lemons.

Tanner ignored him, tracing his finger over a ravine. There.

He looked up at the instructor. "Best route is north by northeast, keeping elevation low along the ridgeline. It'll give us cover and keep us off the main trails."

The captain studied him for a beat, then nodded.

"Correct. Move out."

Tanner shoved his map back in his pocket and stood.

Lemons smirked. "Took you long enough."

Tanner shouldered past him without a word.

\*\*\*

Four hours of silence, marching, exhaustion.

Then—gunfire.

Simulated rounds cracked through the trees, snapping overhead as Tanner and his team dived for cover.

"AMBUSH!" someone shouted.

Tanner rolled behind a log, gripping his rifle tight. Through the dim red haze of his night vision, he could see enemy silhouettes moving fast.

They had been waiting for them.

Hell Night wasn't just an endurance event.

It was a war.

Tanner spoke fast, pointing toward cover.

"Smith, Harris—flank left. Lay down suppressing fire."

The two cadets broke off, moving low through the brush.

Tanner turned to Lemons.

"You got a plan, Captain America?" Lemons muttered, breath heavy but steady.

Tanner didn't hesitate. "Yeah. Try not to get shot."

Lemons snorted. "Funny."

Then—they moved together, sweeping right, keeping low as they returned fire.

Tanner aimed precisely, tagging a silhouette in the chest.

Lemons dropped another.

The "enemy" force fell back, realizing they'd lost momentum.

Tanner exhaled the weight on his chest lifting—just for a second.

Then came the real test.

***

They barely had time to regroup before the next challenge hit them.

"Your mission is simple. Retrieve the VIP."

Tanner stood among the remaining cadets, heart still pounding as the instructor laid out the scenario.

"She's held in a secure facility. Heavily guarded. Minimal intel. You have to find a way in, retrieve her, and get her to the extraction point before enemy reinforcements arrive."

Tanner gritted his teeth.

This was it. The final test.

And his team?

Lemons was on it.

Of course.

***

Tanner led half the team, while Lemons took the other half.

"We split. You cause a distraction at the front. We slip in through the east side."

Lemons' eyes flickered, assessing. Then he nodded.

"Try not to trip over your own feet, Tanner."

Tanner smirked. "I'll let you know when I need your advice."

Lemons just rolled his eyes and moved off.

Tanner led his team low through the brush, keeping their footsteps silent.

The facility came into view—a small wooden structure, likely an old training building repurposed for the test.

Two "guards" stood out front, scanning the woods.

Tanner motioned for silence.

Then, from the other side of the compound—gunfire.

Lemons' team had engaged.

The guards turned.

Tanner moved fast.

One guard went down with a quick, precise shot.

The other barely had time to react before Tanner's team swarmed the entrance.

They were in.

\*\*\*

Tanner found the VIP tied to a chair in the back room—a female instructor playing the part.

He cut the ties fast, hauling her up.

"We have to move. Now."

Outside, the gunfire intensified.

Lemons' voice crackled over the radio. "Reinforcements coming your way, Tanner. You better hustle."

Tanner clenched his jaw. They weren't going to make it to extraction in time.

Unless—

His eyes landed on a supply truck parked outside the compound.

A way out.

Tanner clicked his radio.

"Lemons, I need you to cover the road. We're taking the truck."

A pause.

Then—"That's risky as hell."

"So's getting caught. Can you cover or not?"

A beat. Then—"Fine. But if you crash it, I'm telling everyone you can't drive."**

Tanner grinned despite himself.

"Noted. Moving now."

He shoved the VIP into the truck, hopping into the driver's seat.

Lemons' team lit up the road, suppressing fire and giving them cover.

Tanner slammed the gas.

The truck tore down the dirt road, kicking up a cloud of dust behind it.

Minutes later, the extraction point came into view.

Tanner hit the brakes, skidding to a stop.

The VIP was safe.

And just like that—

Hell Night was over.

***

Tanner staggered out of the truck, every inch of his body aching, exhausted, and drenched in sweat.

Lemons was waiting, arms crossed.

For a second, they just stared at each other.

Then Lemons muttered, "Not bad, Tanner."

Tanner snorted. "Not bad yourself."

Lemons smirked. "Try to keep up next time."

Tanner chuckled. "Right back at you."

And for once, it wasn't a taunt.

It was respect.

Hell Night had tried to break them.

But they were still standing.

# CHAPTER 16

## GRADUATION

The parade ground was still, the early morning sun casting long shadows across the freshly pressed uniforms of the newly commissioned officers. Rows of cadets stood at attention, their chests swelled with the weight of accomplishment.

Chris Tanner felt the tightness in his throat, the kind that came with knowing he had survived, fought, and earned his place here.

The past weeks had pushed him to his limits. He had faced down his failures, won battles in the barracks and the field, and for the first time, he wasn't standing in Drew Lemons' shadow.

Lemons was there, of course, standing a few rows over, but something had changed between them. Maybe it was respect. Maybe just the acknowledgment that Tanner wasn't someone he could push aside anymore.

But right now, none of that mattered.

The officer at the podium continued his speech, but Tanner barely heard the words. All he could think about was the weight of his commission papers in his hands and the future waiting beyond this ceremony.

Then, as the final orders were given, the entire class shouted in unison:

"Sir, yes, sir!"

The ceremony ended, and the cadets burst into celebration—handshakes, slaps on the back, shouts of relief.

Tanner let out a deep breath. It was over.

Or so he thought.

Tanner was making his way across the yard when he saw her.

Captain Alison Scott.

She stood near the edge of the field, arms crossed, watching him with the same calculating gaze she had worn back during his stress interview.

Tanner stiffened.

This wasn't a casual visit.

Scott never did casual.

He walked over and saluted. "Ma'am."

She returned the salute but didn't immediately speak. Instead, she handed him a sealed envelope.

"Your orders, Tanner."

Tanner blinked. He had expected a standard unit assignment—somewhere stateside, maybe a deployment overseas.

But when he opened the envelope, his brow furrowed.

"Pine Gap, Australia?"

Scott's lips curved slightly, but there was no amusement in her eyes.

"That's right. Report immediately. Further details will be provided upon arrival."

Tanner's head snapped up.

"Australia? Pine Gap?!"

Scott just shrugged. "Welcome to the real military, Lieutenant. You're about to find out how deep the rabbit hole goes."

Tanner's pulse quickened.

Something about this felt different.

This wasn't just another assignment.

It was the start of something much bigger.

And he had a feeling it was only the beginning.

# CHAPTER 17

## THE CAVE OF ECHOES

The air inside the cave was heavy, ancient, and alive.

Agent Trinity Lemma moved carefully, her boots barely making a sound against the uneven stone floor. The weight of her covert infiltration pressed on her shoulders, but she ignored it.

Her headlamp flickered, sending beams of white light over the cavern walls.

Markings.

They stretched across the stone, vast and intricate, etched deep into the rock like a script frozen in time. This wasn't natural.

And if her instincts were right, it wasn't native to the planet's inhabitants, either.

She wasn't supposed to be here.

The rest of her team was miles away, stationed outside the main entrance to the cave system. Officially, they were waiting for clearance to begin surveying the ruins.

Unofficially?

Lemma had slipped away the moment no one was looking.

The deeper she went, the less reliable her comms became. Static cut through her earpiece, drowning out the occasional check-in request from her team.

She doubted they'd hear her if she responded.

At least, that's what she told herself.

Because if they did?

They'd drag her back before she could figure out what this place really was.

\*\*\*

Lemma reached out, her gloved fingers tracing the markings.

She could feel the indentations, the purpose behind each carved line.

This was a language—she was sure of it.

She lifted her datapad, snapping images and feeding them into a translation program.

The results were frustratingly empty.

She sighed. No direct matches.

But then she overlaid Sumerian cuneiform and something clicked.

The symbols weren't an exact match, but the patterns, the structure—they were too close to be coincidence.

This civilization, whoever they were, had left a message.

A warning, maybe.

Or a key to something even bigger.

Her heart pounded with the weight of discovery.

She'd spent her life chasing history, searching for the whispers of the past buried beneath time.

This was more than she had ever dreamed.

But something about this place felt wrong.

Like she was being watched.

Or worse—like she wasn't alone.

\*\*\*

The silence in the cavern was thick—the kind that pressed in from all sides, swallowing even the sound of her own breath.

Then—a deep, distant rumble.

Lemma froze.

Not a tremor.

Not a cave-in.

This was different.

It sounded like movement.

From an adjacent cavern.

Her pulse quickened, every instinct firing at once.

It wasn't just one noise—it was a series of them. Heavy. Rhythmic. Deliberate.

Something was in here with her.

Lemma took a slow, careful step back, her boot barely making contact with the stone.

Her comm earpiece crackled with static.

Useless.

She clenched her jaw. Think.

This wasn't the first time she'd been in a place she shouldn't be.

She knew how to get out of trouble.

Slow, steady breathing. Quiet, controlled movements. No sudden noise.

The sound of shifting rock echoed again, this time closer.

The hair on the back of her neck stood on end.

Whatever it was, it was big.

And it was awake.

# CHAPTER 18

## INTO THE UNKNOWN

Lemma moved carefully, pressing herself against the cold stone wall as she listened to the heavy, deliberate movement coming from the adjacent cavern.

It wasn't an echo.

It wasn't a rockfall.

Something was in here with her.

Her instinct screamed at her to leave, but she wasn't ready to go back—not yet. Not when she was standing in a place untouched by time, filled with markings that could change everything they thought they knew.

She had risked too much sneaking in alone to walk away now.

But she needed distance.

And fast.

Her boots made almost no noise as she slid away from the wall and moved deeper into the cave.

She kept her headlamp dim, casting only a faint glow ahead.

The last thing she wanted was to draw attention.

The cavern opened up ahead, splitting into two tunnels—one wide and jagged, the other narrow and smooth.

The rumbling noise behind her shifted, followed by a faint, low vibration through the stone.

It was getting closer.

She forced herself to breathe evenly, analyzing her options.

The wider tunnel looked like the obvious choice—more space, easier to maneuver.

But the narrow tunnel was better. Tighter. More defensible.

And if whatever was following her was big?

It wouldn't fit.

She took the narrow path, angling her shoulders to squeeze through the passage.

The walls felt unnaturally smooth as if something had shaped them rather than erosion.

Her fingers brushed faint indentations in the stone, and her heart pounded faster.

More markings.

\*\*\*

The passage opened into a small chamber, barely large enough for her to stand upright.

And on the walls—

More carvings.

She swallowed, reaching for her datapad and snapping images as quickly as she could.

Unlike the markings from before, these were more structured, almost resembling a timeline.

There were figures, strange and elongated, clustered together.

Above them—what looked like a star shifting, distorting.

And below—

Her breath caught.

One symbol stood out from the rest.

It was clearer and more defined than the others.

It was Sumerian.

An ancient, forgotten word.

"Exodus."

Her mind raced.

Who had written this?

Who had been here before her?

And what were they running from?

\*\*\*

The ground trembled beneath her boots.

The movement from the adjacent cavern had stopped.

A deep, guttural exhalation vibrated through the rock—so low it was almost beyond hearing.

Lemma's blood ran cold.

Whatever it was, it was close.

It wasn't moving randomly.

It was searching.

For her.

She turned off her headlamp, plunging herself into darkness.

The only light came from the faint blue glow of her datapad screen.

Her breathing slowed.

Every instinct told her to stay absolutely still.

She wasn't alone in this cave.

And she had just gone too deep to turn back.

# CHAPTER 19

## THE GATHERING BELOW

Silence.

Lemma remained perfectly still, pressed against the cold stone wall, her breathing shallow.

The low vibrations from the cavern behind her had stopped, but that didn't bring her any comfort.

It meant whoever—or whatever—was searching for her had paused.

And that was worse.

A hunting animal didn't stop unless it was listening.

Or unless it knew exactly where its prey was.

She needed to move. Now.

\*\*\*

Slowly, she shifted her weight forward, placing each step with precision to avoid kicking loose gravel.

The tunnel she had squeezed into was too confined, and if she was cornered here, there'd be no way to fight back.

The walls narrowed again ahead, but beyond them, she could see a faint light—a deeper opening.

An exit.

Or at least, a way out of this tight passage.

Her comms crackled briefly, a burst of static in her earpiece.

Then—nothing.

She tried not to let that rattle her.

She had known the moment she entered the deeper tunnels that her connection to the surface was fragile at best.

Right now, her mission was simple.

Get out. Get clear. Regroup.

She moved faster now, staying low, barely breathing, her hand drifting over the cave wall to guide herself.

Then—her foot caught the edge of a loose rock.

It tumbled forward, bouncing down the narrow passage.

Each impact sent echoes rippling through the tunnel.

Lemma froze.

The air itself felt like it held its breath.

Then—movement.

The sound of something shifting, adjusting, turning toward the noise.

A second later—a deep, guttural clicking sound.

It was close.

Too close.

She didn't wait.

She bolted.

\*\*\*

Lemma forced herself through the narrowing walls, feeling the stone scrape against her shoulders as she pushed through.

Her heart pounded like a drum, but she didn't slow down.

The light ahead was growing stronger, casting long, jagged shadows against the walls.

She squeezed through one final, tight gap—

And then suddenly, she was free.

The passage opened abruptly, the floor sloping downward, loose dust swirling around her boots.

She barely had time to register the shift in space before she stumbled forward—

And stopped dead.

Her eyes widened.

She had found an overlook.

A massive opening in the cave system stretched before her, revealing a vast, unfathomably large cavern below.

She instinctively pressed herself flat against the rocky ledge, breath caught in her throat.

Because down below—

A large group had gathered.

Dozens, maybe hundreds.

Standing in eerie, disciplined silence.

They weren't facing her.

They were all looking in the same direction— toward a raised stone platform in the center of the cavern.

A stage.

And for the first time since entering these caves, Lemma realized she wasn't just intruding on ruins.

She had walked straight into something alive.

Something active.

Something she wasn't meant to see.

\*\*\*

The figures stood completely still, all their attention locked on the platform.

Even from her hidden vantage point, Lemma could see subtle differences between them.

Some were taller, their bodies draped in dark, flowing robes. Others had armor—faintly metallic, almost organic in design.

This wasn't a casual meeting.

This was an assembly. A ritual.

The stone platform at the center was old, its edges smoothed by time, worn by use.

But what stood upon it was new.

A towering pillar, pulsing with an unnatural blue-green glow, its light casting long shadows over the gathered figures.

And next to it—

A single individual stood, arms raised.

They spoke, but from this distance, Lemma couldn't hear the words.

She barely dared to breathe.

She had spent her life deciphering ancient texts, trying to reconstruct voices long silenced by time.

But this—

This was history in motion.

Not something long dead.

Something very much alive.

And she was watching it unfold in real-time.

\*\*\*

Her mind raced with possibilities.

Who were they?

Why were they here, so deep beneath the surface?

And—most importantly—

Had they heard her enter?

Lemma swallowed hard.

She had managed to avoid whatever had been hunting her in the tunnels.

But now she faced a much bigger problem.

Because even from here, she could tell—

Whoever these people were, they weren't alone.

And whatever was happening on that stage…

It was only just beginning.

# CHAPTER 20

## ARRIVAL AT PINE GAP

The heat hit him first.

Tanner stepped off the transport plane into the blazing Australian sun, squinting against the brightness.

The desert stretched for miles in every direction, a vast nothingness of red sand and scattered scrub.

And in the middle of it all—Pine Gap.

From the outside, it looked like just another military installation, a collection of low-slung buildings, communication arrays, and a security perimeter thick with armed guards.

But Tanner knew better.

Because you didn't get sent to Pine Gap for just any mission.

You got sent here because you weren't coming back the same.

***

A black SUV waited just off the airstrip, engine idling.

Tanner threw his duffel into the back and climbed inside, shutting the door behind him with a solid thunk.

Seated beside him in the dimly lit back seat was Captain Scott.

Unlike the fresh recruits at OCS, Tanner had never made the mistake of underestimating her.

Scott wasn't just another officer—she was the second-in-command of one of the most classified operations on the planet.

And she had been grooming him for this moment.

At the wheel, a young airman in standard fatigues focused straight ahead, hands at ten and two, his expression unreadable.

Scott barely looked up from the tablet in her hands, flicking through files with the same calm precision she always had.

She finally glanced at Tanner, giving him a once-over.

"You look like hell, Lieutenant."

Tanner smirked. "Good to see you too, ma'am."

Scott didn't return the smile. She never did. Instead, she handed him the tablet.

"Then let's see if you're ready."

Tanner took the device, scanning the image on the screen.

And then he froze.

It wasn't a map.

It wasn't a document.

It was a planet.

***

The atmosphere in the SUV changed.

Tanner stared at the massive, unfamiliar world on the screen.

Its surface was a mix of harsh deserts and sprawling dark oceans, partially obscured by swirling storm clouds.

"You're telling me this isn't Earth."

Scott nodded.

"Correct."

The airman in the front seat didn't react.

If he knew what they were talking about, he was well-trained enough to keep his mouth shut.

The SUV slowed, approaching a restricted hangar near the edge of the compound.

Tanner exhaled sharply, forcing his mind to catch up.

"You've been pulling my strings since day one."

Scott smirked, just barely.

"Not pulling. Preparing."

Tanner glanced out the window. The base had layers—outer security, administrative offices, comms infrastructure. But where they were headed?

This was something else.

"Say it straight, ma'am. Why am I here?"

Scott tapped the tablet.

"Because you're leading a team off-world."

Tanner let out a short laugh—more reflex than amusement.

"Come again?"

"You heard me."

The vehicle pulled up to a security checkpoint, where a pair of armed guards gave Scott a brief nod before allowing them through.

Scott turned back to Tanner.

"You're here because we need someone who can lead under extreme pressure. Someone who can make the hard calls when things go sideways."

Tanner exhaled slowly.

"That part, I figured. But 'off-world' wasn't in the fine print."

Scott smirked slightly,

"Welcome to the classified side of the job."

\*\*\*

The SUV rolled through a secondary security gate, leading to a massive underground facility carved into the bedrock.

As the doors opened, Tanner's first thought was that it looked nothing like a conventional airbase.

Because it wasn't.

Rows of sleek, aircraft-like vessels lined the underground hangar—except they weren't standard jets.

They were something else entirely.

The designs were unfamiliar, their surfaces dark and seamless, lacking the riveted panels of traditional aircraft.

They looked... smooth. Organic.

Tanner stepped forward, his eyes locked on the nearest vessel.

It hovered—not resting on landing gear, but suspended inches above the ground, completely motionless.

He turned to Scott.

"This is... not Air Force tech."

Scott simply nodded.

"Not entirely."

Tanner exhaled. "Reverse-engineered?"

"Decades in the making."

Tanner ran a hand over the cool, metal-like surface of the nearest craft. It felt strange, neither warm nor cold, like it didn't fully belong in this world.

Scott continued.

"Every major UFO incident you've ever heard of? Roswell, Rendlesham, Kecksburg, Phoenix Lights? Those weren't hoaxes."

Tanner glanced back at her.

Scott smirked. "We've been borrowing ideas for a long time."

\*\*\*

Scott led him into a briefing room, where a woman in military uniform stood waiting—Colonel Everett.

She didn't waste time.

"Lieutenant Tanner, we're sending you and a handpicked team off-world to investigate a growing situation."

She gestured to the largest projection on the wall— a planetary map.

It was the same world from the tablet, but now he could see regions marked in red.

"We've established limited contact with the inhabitants. But a recent shift in the planetary environment has led to unrest, and we believe an extremist faction is using it as leverage."

Tanner's eyes narrowed. "What kind of unrest?"

Everett crossed her arms.

"Solar instability. Their sun is shifting phase, and a radical group believes we're responsible."

Tanner let that sink in.

Everett studied him for a moment before adding, "Your background in environmental engineering and... certain research you did in college might prove useful here."

Tanner blinked.

"You're saying research I did in college is somehow relevant here?"

Everett smirked. "Let's just say we don't put people in places like this by accident."

Tanner let out a sharp exhale.

"Let me get this straight. You want me to go to an alien world, deal with a planetary crisis, and defuse a religious war."

Scott smirked. "Pretty much."

Tanner glanced at the projection again.

"Who am I working with?"

Everett handed him a classified personnel file.

The name on the first page caught his attention.

Agent Trinity Lemma.

Tanner frowned.

"A linguist?"

Everett nodded.

"She's already there. Last report said she was investigating ancient ruins connected to the sun's activity. But we've lost direct contact."

Tanner shut the file.

"So part of my job is finding her."

Scott leaned against the table.

"You're not just leading a mission, Tanner. You're stepping into something bigger than either of us."

An impossible mission.

A world that wasn't his.

And a team that already needed saving.

Scott stood, her voice even.

"Welcome to Pine Gap."

# CHAPTER 21

## ASSEMBLING EAGLE EIGHT

Tanner stepped into the briefing room, a sterile, windowless chamber filled with classified dossiers, holographic projections of planetary maps, and tactical equipment laid out in meticulous order.

The air was thick with tension, the kind that came before a mission where everyone knew the risks but couldn't speak them aloud.

Six individuals were already inside, standing at ease but watching him closely.

These were the people he'd be leading off-world.

Scott motioned to the group.

"Lieutenant Tanner, meet your team—Eagle Eight."

\*\*\*

Scott gestured to the first man, tall, built like a brawler, but with the sharpest eyes in the room.

"Sergeant First Class Ryan Hale, Special Operations. Ground unit leader."

Hale gave a curt nod, his posture military-perfect. His arms were scarred, his uniform worn, and his expression unreadable.

"Sir."

Scott moved on.

"Lieutenant Sofia Alvarez, combat engineer. Specializes in environmental adaptability and structural assessment."

Alvarez, a lean, no-nonsense woman with dark hair pulled into a tight bun, studied Tanner like she was measuring him.

"Hope you don't mind getting your boots dirty, sir. It's gonna be messy."

"Never minded a little dirt," Tanner said, keeping his tone neutral.

Scott nodded, moving to the next.

"Corporal Darius 'D' Mercer. Communications and cyber-warfare expert."

Mercer, a stocky man with a half-smirk and an undeniable hacker vibe, leaned against the table, arms crossed.

"Nice to see we finally got a new guy. You look like you can actually run, which is an improvement over our last CO."

Tanner raised a brow. "What happened to him?"

Mercer shrugged. "Retired. With a limp."

Tanner didn't ask further.

Scott's eyes shifted to the next member.

A man who didn't quite fit the military mold.

His uniform was clean, but the way he stood—more relaxed, more academic—made him stand out.

"Dr. Elias Vance. Astrophysics and energy systems expert. You're going to want to listen to him when it comes to the tech."

Vance nodded, pushing up his glasses.

"Lieutenant. I assume you've been briefed on the situation."

Tanner folded his arms. "Enough to know we're about to be in the deep end."

Vance smirked. "Then let's get you caught up."

Scott turned toward the last two members.

"Warrant Officer Cole Maddox. Pilot. If you want to get back in one piece, you better keep him happy."

Maddox, a wiry man with gray creeping into his short hair, leaned back in his chair, arms crossed.

"Long as you don't get me shot down, we won't have any problems."

Tanner nodded. "Fair deal."

Scott moved to the final member, a woman who had been standing quietly near the corner of the room.

"Specialist Erin Park. Reconnaissance and stealth operations. She's your forward scout."

Park, short but built for speed, her dark eyes sharp and alert, gave a quick nod.

"I work best alone, but I'll make an exception."

Tanner smirked. "Appreciate that."

Scott glanced at the empty seat at the table.

"Agent Lemma will round out the team. She's already on the ground."

Tanner exhaled, letting the weight of the introductions settle.

Seven people. His responsibility.

This wasn't just an insertion team. It was Eagle Eight.

And he was its final piece.

*** 

Scott motioned toward a holographic display, where a sleek, matte-black craft rotated in midair.

Tanner's eyes locked on it.

It wasn't a fighter jet.

It wasn't a shuttle.

It was something in between.

"This is the SR-12 Phantom. Our means of interstellar travel, based on decades of reverse-engineered technology."

Vance tapped a console, and the display shifted, showing the propulsion core—a non-traditional drive system with an eerie, pulsating glow.

"We call it a Gravimetric Displacement Drive. Not quite faster-than-light, but close enough. Uses localized gravitational fields to fold space, allowing near-instantaneous jumps between distant points. There is no need for hyperspace lanes and no wormholes. Just point, calculate, and shift."

Tanner nodded slowly, absorbing it.

"How precise are the jumps?"

"That's why we have me," Vance said, tapping his temple. "It's not perfect. If we miscalculate, we end up inside a mountain. Or worse."

"Good to know," Tanner muttered.

The display changed again, this time showing armor schematics and weapons load-outs.

Scott took over.

"Our suits are equipped with adaptive shielding, nanocomposite plating, and full environmental sealing."

Alvarez spoke up.

"It's not quite power armor, but it'll take a hit. And if we're in a vacuum, hostile atmosphere, or knee-deep in acid rain, we won't suffocate."

Tanner glanced at the display. The designs were sleek, almost too advanced for human technology.

Scott picked up a compact rifle from the table and handed it to him.

"M-9 Valkyrie. Fires standard kinetic rounds, but it's also equipped with an EM charge module to disrupt shielding and electronics. Good against anything trying to fry you before you fry them."

Tanner tested the weight, nodding approvingly.

"Sidearm?"

Mercer grinned and tossed him a smaller, angular pistol.

"Meet the Talon. Gauss-powered, fires metal slugs at Mach speeds. You'll like it."

Tanner caught it smoothly, giving it a quick once-over before holstering it.

Scott watched him. "Satisfied?"

Tanner exhaled. "Not even a little. But at least now I know what I'm dying in."

The team chuckled, but the tension in the room remained.

Because they all knew what was coming.

***

The room dimmed, and a new planetary image appeared on the holo-display.

The world they were heading to.

Scott's voice was measured and controlled.

"Mission parameters are simple. Get in, stabilize the situation, and recover Agent Lemma."

Tanner nodded.

"And if the situation is beyond saving?"

Scott met his gaze.

"Then we contain it. Whatever it takes."

Silence hung in the air.

Then Mercer clapped his hands.

"Well, I don't know about you all, but I was planning on surviving this mission. So let's get to work."

Tanner smirked.

This was his team.

And their mission was about to begin.

Scott stepped forward, voice steady.

"Wheels up in 24 hours. Get prepped."

She turned to Tanner.

"Welcome to Eagle Eight."

# CHAPTER 22

## PREPPING FOR DEPLOYMENT

The clock was running down. Twenty-four hours until wheels up.

Tanner knew this mission was unlike any he'd ever trained for. It wasn't just about combat, survival, or leadership—it was about navigating the unknown. And that meant understanding the people, the team, and the science before they left.

He had three meetings to knock out before deployment.

First, Captain Scott.

Then, Lieutenant Alvarez.

And finally, Dr. Vance.

Each one was critical.

Each one could mean the difference between success and failure.

***

Scott's office was as no-nonsense as she was—bare walls, a desk covered in mission files, and a single chair for visitors. Tanner stepped inside, closing the door behind him.

Scott didn't look up from her tablet.

"Take a seat, Tanner. We need to talk about Ambassador Ladrinen and your first priority after landing."

Tanner lowered himself into the chair. "Finding Lemma."

Scott's eyes flicked up. "Yes, but there's a complication."

Tanner leaned forward. "Of course there is."

Scott tapped the tablet, bringing up a holographic image of an alien figure with sharp, reptilian features and piercing yellow eyes. His posture was regal, draped in ceremonial armor, the markings on his chest suggesting status, authority.

"Ladrinen is the official representative of the Unified Clans. He's been working with us cautiously, and his people expect an authorized research team to arrive soon."

Tanner frowned. "And Lemma's not part of that team?"

Scott shook her head.

"She was inserted ahead of the main group with a small advance party. They're already at the site, waiting for final clearance to begin their survey."

Tanner exhaled sharply. "And Ladrinen doesn't know?"

Scott leaned forward. "As far as he's concerned, Lemma is still with the main delegation. He assumes she'll be arriving with them."

Tanner ran a hand down his face. "So we have an advance team sitting in a highly sensitive zone, completely unsanctioned, and they don't know the locals have no idea they're there?"

Scott nodded. "Exactly. If Ladrinen finds out, he might see it as an act of deception. At best, we damage our relationship. At worst, we give the Mana faction all the proof they need to turn the population against us."

Tanner exhaled through his nose. "And my job is to recover Lemma before anyone realizes we played fast and loose with the rules?"

Scott smirked. "Now you're getting it."

Tanner leaned back, arms crossed. "And if she's already been made?"

Scott's smirk faded.

"Then this mission gets a lot more complicated."

Tanner let out a slow breath.

"Fantastic. Anything else I should know?"

Scott tapped the planetary map, zooming in on the mountainous capital city.

"Ladrinen is based in Var'leth. He's the key to maintaining order, and if things go south, we need him on our side. He'll be expecting you to coordinate with him once you're on the ground."

Tanner nodded, filing that away.

"So, first objective: recover Lemma. Second objective: keep Ladrinen in the dark. Third objective: don't start an interstellar war."

Scott smirked again. "Sounds about right."

Tanner let out a long sigh.

"Welcome to command," Scott added.

***

Tanner found Lieutenant Sofia Alvarez in one of the armory prep rooms, adjusting her gear. The combat engineer's expression was sharp and focused, and when she saw him step in, she gestured toward the array of weapons laid out.

"You here for gear checks or to figure out how we don't kill each other out there?" she asked, adjusting a harness on her chest rig.

Tanner crossed his arms. "Both, ideally. But let's start with the team. Anything I need to know before we drop into a warzone together?"

Alvarez leaned against the table, smirking.

"Hale's solid. You won't get a better field lead, but we call him 'Salty Dog.'"

Tanner raised a brow. "Why?"

"He puts salt on everything. Steak, eggs, coffee—hell, I caught him dumping it in protein shakes once."

Tanner frowned. "Okay, but why?"

Alvarez chuckled. "Something about an argument with his ex-wife. You'll have to ask him for the full story, but let's just say, when he got divorced, salt won."

Tanner smirked. "Noted. And Mercer?"

Alvarez rolled her eyes. "Wild card. If something electronic needs hacking, breaking, or reverse-engineering, he's your guy. Just don't expect him to salute while he does it."

"Maddox?"

Alvarez exhaled, shaking her head.

"Best pilot we've got. But he's… colorful. Half the time, you'll swear he's not taking anything seriously, but when it counts, he delivers. Just brace yourself—he thinks he's funnier than he is."

As if on cue, Maddox's voice boomed from down the hall.

"Hey! If anyone touches my seat adjustments, I will personally make sure you have the most uncomfortable ride of your life!"

Alvarez smirked. "See what I mean?"

Tanner sighed. "We have a comedian in the cockpit."

"Hey, don't knock it. If we're all about to die, at least he'll make us laugh first."

Tanner shook his head. "Alright. What about Park?"

Alvarez exhaled. "She's quiet, but she'll get the job done. You won't see her when she's working, and that's how it should be. Just trust that she's handling business."

Tanner nodded. "And you?"

Alvarez raised a brow. "You tell me, sir. You're the one leading us."

Tanner let the moment stretch before he spoke.

"I lead from the front. I don't waste lives. But I don't hesitate when the call needs to be made. Can you work with that?"

Alvarez studied him for a long moment.

Then, finally, she nodded.

"Yeah. That'll work."

*** 

The science lab was filled with data projections, planetary models, and complex waveforms Tanner didn't have the expertise to fully decipher.

Dr. Elias Vance was at the center of it, hunched over a console, muttering calculations under his breath.

Tanner knocked on the edge of the metal table. "Tell me something good, Doc."

Vance looked up, adjusting his glasses. "That depends on how you define 'good.'"

Tanner exhaled. "What do we know about the sun's phase shift? Anything useful?"

Vance straightened, gesturing toward a holographic representation of the alien star system. The sun was marked in fluctuating colors, energy readings shifting in unpredictable patterns.

"It's not just shifting phases—it's destabilizing in a way we don't fully understand. The local civilizations have records of past fluctuations, but nothing like this. If we don't find a way to counteract the changes, their entire planet could become uninhabitable."

Tanner narrowed his eyes. "Any solutions?"

Vance hesitated.

"Not yet. But we're running out of time to figure it out."

Tanner exhaled sharply.

"Fantastic."

***

By the time Tanner left the lab, the weight of command was fully on his shoulders.

He had his team.

He had his mission.

And in less than a day, they'd be stepping onto an alien world with no guarantees of coming back.

Tanner clenched his jaw.

Whatever was waiting for them out there, Eagle Eight would be ready.

# CHAPTER 23

## THE RALLYING CRY

Lemma pressed herself against the damp, uneven rock, heart hammering in her chest. The air in the cavern was thick, stale with the scent of damp earth and ancient decay. Somewhere below, the crowd continued to roar, their voices a frenzied mix of praise and anger.

She had followed the sound carefully, moving deeper into the labyrinth of tunnels, each step deliberate. Now, she was close enough to hear the words clearly.

And what she heard sent a cold knot of dread into her stomach.

\*\*\*

Below her, in a massive hollowed-out cavern, a chaplain stood at a small podium, arms raised to the crowd. His voice boomed, filling the cavern walls, his words laced with conviction and fury.

"They told us to listen to the science. But they lied to us."

The crowd erupted, their cheers bouncing off the stone, making the cavern feel smaller, more suffocating.

Lemma gritted her teeth.

"It is the scientists and their new allies that have angered our Lord. That is why our sun has shifted phases. They are the reason our atmosphere has become toxic. It is their fault our crops will no longer grow and our animals are dying."

Damn it.

It was worse than she thought. The Mana faction wasn't just blaming outsiders, they were weaponizing faith against scientific reality. And now, with the sun's destabilization worsening, they were looking for someone to blame.

"The scientists and their lies are why we have been forced underground. Your children are suffering because of them. They are the cause of the suffering that our elderly are forced to endure."

The chaplain placed a hand on his chest, then extended his arms outward, his voice rising.

"We, too, are suffering. Our God has been greatly offended. But we can change that. We can expose their lies. We must rise up against those who have wronged our Lord. We are ready to fight, we are ready to die to defend our God."

The crowd responded in kind, their voices unified, echoing through the tunnels like rolling thunder.

The chaplain's voice softened, reverent.

"Let us pray. Lord, we thank you for the blessings that you have given us. We ask that you grant our commanders the wisdom to overcome our foes. We ask that you fill our fighters with the courage and strength to charge into battle. We ask all these things in the name of the Father, Son, and Holy Spirit. Amen."

The crowd erupted once more, hands raised, voices a mix of praise and fervor.

Lemma barely heard them. Her mind was reeling.

The Holy Trinity.

Father, Son, and Holy Spirit.

The phrasing was almost identical to Christian doctrine—but how? The reptilian inhabitants of this planet had no recorded connection to Earth, no known cultural overlap. And yet, here they were, echoing words she had grown up hearing in church.

And her own name. Trinity.

Coincidence? Or something deeper?

Focus. She didn't have time to question it now. But she wouldn't forget it.

The chaplain stepped back, gesturing toward another figure.

"Commander, please come. Lead us into battle. We are ready."

***

A new voice took over, deeper, authoritative, cutting through the noise.

"Thank you, chaplain."

A commander stepped to the podium, his presence alone commanding respect. The room fell into anticipatory silence.

"We have a difficult job ahead of us."

Lemma shifted carefully, pressing closer, making sure she didn't lose a single word.

"The substation tucked in the side of this hill is essential to their operations. We must take over and shut down this energy plant."

She barely stopped herself from cursing aloud.

They weren't just preparing for battle—they had a target. And if the Mana faction seized the energy plant, it could cripple the region's infrastructure.

The commander continued.

"Because we will be coming under the cover of darkness, we have the element of surprise. But once the first wave engages, that advantage will be gone. We expect to encounter significant resistance. This is why we will quickly advance the second wave. We anticipate that once the second wave joins the first, they will capitulate."

"But we will hold the third wave in the rear as reinforcements if needed. Now kit up, head out, and let's get it."

The room exploded with cheers, soldiers raising weapons, the air thick with violent anticipation.

***

Lemma backed away carefully, moving silently, ensuring she didn't dislodge loose rock or make a sound.

This was bad.

Very bad.

She needed to warn Eagle Eight.

If they landed without knowing what was happening, they wouldn't just be stepping into a diplomatic crisis—they'd be stepping onto an active battlefield.

She turned, moving quickly, making her way back toward the tunnels.

She had to find a way to reach them.

Before it was too late.

# CHAPTER 24

## THE DESCENT

There was no time.

Lemma moved quickly, retracing her steps through the winding tunnels of the cave. Every instinct in her body screamed at her to hurry. If the Mana faction moved on the energy plant, everything could unravel.

She needed to reach her team. She needed to warn Eagle Eight.

Her mind raced through the best route back to the surface, the safest way to move undetected—but adrenaline made her reckless. Her boots scraped against loose rock, and she didn't hear the soft crumble until it was too late.

The floor gave way beneath her.

The world tilted, gravity taking over as she tumbled downward.

She tried to grab at anything—a ledge, a jagged rock, something—but her fingers only scraped against dust and smooth stone.

Then she hit the incline.

Her body slammed into the rocky slope, her momentum carrying her down at a punishing speed. Pain ignited in her side, her ribs screaming in protest as she twisted, tumbling end over end.

Her left leg smashed into an unseen outcrop, and a bolt of agony shot through her as her ankle wrenched at an unnatural angle.

She barely had time to register the pain before she collided hard with the cavern floor, the impact driving the air from her lungs.

Everything went dark for a second.

Then, the pain crashed over her in full.

Her ribs ached with every shallow breath, a stabbing sensation lancing through her side. Her leg throbbed violently, and when she tried to shift it, a sharp, searing pain locked her in place.

She had fallen into another cavern.

And she was trapped.

\*\*\*

The cavern around her was eerily silent, the echoes of her fall settling into a deep, oppressive stillness. Dust and loose sediment still drifted in the air, stirred from where her body had slammed into the rock.

She forced herself to breathe, though each inhale was ragged and shallow. Assess the damage.

Her ribs—probably cracked.

Her left leg—definitely injured.

Every movement set her nerves on fire.

Not good.

Through the pain, she became aware of something strange.

The walls of the cavern weren't smooth, nor were they naturally eroded like the others she had passed through. Instead, they were covered in rows of carefully carved notches, stretching from floor to ceiling.

It wasn't just an ancient design. It was intentional.

She squinted in the dim light, her vision blurry from pain.

Inside each carved notch was a small stone, tucked deliberately within the opening. Some were simple pieces of jagged rock, but others had etched markings, worn from time but still visible.

It looked like… an archival system.

A library carved into the stone.

Despite the pain hammering through her body, a sliver of curiosity cut through her panic. This wasn't the work of the Mana faction—this was older. Much older.

The previous civilization. The ones who had vanished.

She pressed a hand against the cave wall, forcing herself upright, but a fresh wave of agony ripped through her side, leaving her dizzy.

Damn it.

She didn't have time for this.

She needed to get out.

But the walls were too steep to climb, and she didn't see an obvious exit.

Trapped. Injured. Alone.

And the people she needed to warn? They had no idea she was even down here.

Lemma clenched her jaw, forcing back the pain.

She was not going to die in this cave.

One way or another—she was getting out.

# CHAPTER 25

## SIEGE OF THE POWER STATION

The first explosion shattered the silence of the night.

A shockwave rippled through the valley, sending dust and debris raining down on the facility's outer barricades. Sirens blared, cutting through the chaos as the defenders—a mix of local military forces and off-world security personnel—rushed into position.

Inside the Var'leth Power Station, the control room was already a scene of controlled panic.

"Multiple breaches along the southern perimeter!"

"Turret One is offline! We're losing power to the northern grid!"

"We need reinforcements now!"

Commander Julek, the station's head of security, slammed a fist against the console. His reptilian eyes flicked between the monitors, displaying blurred images of the enemy force pressing forward.

The Mana faction had come in force.

Hundreds of them, clad in makeshift armor, weapons scavenged from old arsenals, a mix of ballistic and energy-based arms stolen or smuggled from black markets. They weren't organized like a traditional army, but they didn't need to be.

They fought with zeal. With conviction.

And they were throwing everything they had at the station's defenses.

***

The first wave surged forward, pouring through the broken perimeter, clashing violently with the entrenched defenders.

Gunfire and energy blasts ripped through the night, the defensive positions lighting up as heavy turret emplacements opened fire, mowing down the first line of attackers.

"Hold the line! Hold the damn line!" one of the officers shouted, rallying the defenders as the Mana warriors pressed forward.

Their numbers were staggering, but they had little coordination they attacked in a relentless rush, fanatics willing to die for their cause.

And die they did.

The security forces held firm, cutting them down in waves of gunfire and disciplined counterattacks.

The bodies began to pile up at the choke points. The first wave had failed.

But the defenders knew this wasn't over.

***

A sudden, unnatural hum filled the air.

Julek turned toward the monitors, his scaled brow furrowing. "What the hell is that—"

The second wave came not with foot soldiers, but with artillery.

Explosions tore through the barricades, sending chunks of metal and stone flying. Defensive gun emplacements erupted in fire and smoke, their crews thrown into the air from the force of the blasts.

Then, one of the shells hit the control room.

Everything went white.

A shockwave ripped through the chamber, sending consoles exploding into showers of sparks. The reinforced windows shattered inward, jagged shards slicing through the air like blades.

Julek barely had time to throw himself to the ground before a chunk of the wall tore away, exposing the burning station beyond.

Screams filled the air.

Workers were ripped apart, bodies flung like ragdolls from the force of the blast. Systems short-circuited sparks danced across the floor as flames erupted along the consoles.

Pain blossomed in Julek's side.

His vision swam as he looked down—shrapnel embedded deep in his lower abdomen, blood pooling beneath him.

He clenched his jaw, forcing himself to push through the pain, crawling toward the nearest console that was still functional. His claws slipped against his own blood, but he refused to stop.

Around him, the control room was a wreck—most of the staff were either dead or too injured to fight.

Outside, the Mana faction charged again.

This time, they had cover from the artillery barrage.

And this time, they pushed deeper into the station.

Gunfire roared from every direction.

Defenders fought in the hallways, in the machinery pits, in the elevated control sections that oversaw the power cores.

The station was bleeding personnel.

Still, they held. Barely.

But the battle was turning.

The enemy was inside.

***

Julek's hands were slick with blood, though he couldn't remember if it was his or someone else's. He could barely hear through the constant barrage of gunfire and explosions.

A lieutenant stumbled toward him, gripping a wound at his side.

"We can't take much more of this! The core's containment systems are failing! If we lose another sector—"

A deafening boom cut him off.

The north reactor wing exploded.

Smoke and flame poured from the structure as power flickered throughout the facility.

Warning lights flashed red across every console in the control room.

The station was crumbling.

Julek forced himself to stand, pain lancing through his body, but he kept going. If the station fell, so did the entire region.

Then, just as it seemed they would finally be overrun—

A signal came through the enemy ranks.

A sharp, echoing horn—three long bursts.

The attack stopped.

The Mana faction fighters began to pull back, dragging their wounded, retreating toward the jagged hills that surrounded the station.

They were falling back.

The defenders staggered forward, weapons still raised, too stunned to believe it at first.

Julek forced himself upright, his side burning, blood soaking through his uniform. His voice was hoarse when he spoke into the comms.

"Report. Are they retreating?"

A beat of silence, then:

"Confirmed, sir. They're gone."

Julek let out a slow, shuddering breath.

They had survived.

But barely.

\*\*\*

The station was a ruin.

Bodies littered the halls, the barricades burned and broken, the defensive turrets reduced to scrap.

Inside, the reactor cores flickered, struggling to maintain stability.

A technician approached Julek, wiping blood and soot from his face.

"Sir... we lost too much infrastructure. The station's running at minimal capacity. If we don't get repairs soon... we're looking at total failure."

Julek clenched his jaw, pain radiating from his wounds.

This station was the lifeline of the region. If it failed completely, everything—from military defenses to food production—would collapse.

And the Mana faction knew that.

This wasn't just an attack.

It was the opening move in a much bigger war.

Julek turned his gaze toward the horizon, where the Mana faction's forces had disappeared.

They'd be back.

And next time, there might not be anyone left to stop them.

# CHAPTER 26

## ORDERS IN THE DARK

Tanner stood near the open cargo bay of the transport as it descended toward the surface, his arms crossed, his gaze fixed on the planet below. The capital city stretched in the distance, a mix of alien architecture and military installations, surrounded by rugged terrain.

His mind was elsewhere.

Park.

She was his best scout, and now she had the most dangerous assignment of all.

He turned slightly, scanning the cabin where the rest of Eagle Eight was prepping their gear. Park was strapping down the last of her equipment, her expression unreadable.

"Park, walk with me."

She didn't hesitate. She never did.

As the others continued their final checks, Tanner led her toward the far end of the bay, away from the others. Out of earshot.

"You're breaking off the first chance you get," he said quietly.

She barely blinked. "Copy that."

Tanner exhaled, his voice firm but quiet.

"Lemma and her team haven't checked in for days. If she's in trouble, we need to know."

Park gave a small nod. "Find her. Confirm status. Report back."

"If things go south, don't be a hero."

Park's lips twitched slightly in what might have been a smirk.

"That your job, sir?"

Tanner shook his head.

"I need intel, Park. Not a martyr."

She tightened her gear, adjusting her weapon. "Understood."

Tanner hesitated for half a second, then reached into his side pouch and pulled out a locator beacon. Small, discreet, encrypted to Eagle Eight's comms.

He placed it in her palm.

"If you get compromised, activate this. We'll come running."

She didn't argue. She just secured it into her pack, gave him a single nod, then turned back toward the team.

Tanner watched her go, a sinking feeling settling in his gut.

***

The transport shuddered as it passed through the thin cloud layer, bringing the capital into sharper focus. Below, military and civilian structures intertwined, a city on edge.

"We're on final approach," Maddox called over comms. "ETA three minutes."

Tanner moved toward the cockpit, instinct telling him to get a better look. As he leaned forward, his stomach tightened.

The power station was still burning.

Even from this altitude, he could see the scorched landscape, the billowing smoke, the damaged perimeter. Crews were scrambling to contain the damage, but it was clear—they were losing.

Tanner grabbed the comm unit on his vest.

"Maddox, change course. Take us to the power station."

He hesitated.

"Lieutenant, our orders were to go directly to the capital—"

"We have new orders. Get us down there now."

Tanner turned toward the team, his expression set like stone.

"Change of plans. We're landing at the station. They need help."

Hale frowned. "What about the ambassador?"

"He can wait. This can't."

Nobody argued. They just tightened their gear as the transport banked hard, angling toward the power station.

Tanner could already feel it in his gut.

This wasn't just a detour.

This was the start of something much, much worse.

# CHAPTER 27

## A BATTLE'S AFTERMATH

The transport shuddered as it banked toward the Var'leth Power Station, its thrusters kicking up thick clouds of dust and smoke as it approached. From above, the damage was even worse than Tanner had feared.

The entire southern wall was obliterated, scorched metal twisted into jagged wreckage. Large gaps in the outer defenses left the facility exposed, and what remained of the defensive turrets were little more than burnt-out husks.

Emergency crews were scrambling to contain the fires still burning in the upper reactor wing, their movements desperate and frantic.

And the bodies—

Tanner forced himself not to linger on them.

"Maddox, put us down near the western barricade," he ordered.

"Roger that, Lieutenant. Stand by for drop."

The transport angled sharply, thrusters kicking up dust as it hovered just above the rubble-strewn ground. Before it even fully touched down, Eagle Eight was moving.

"Go! Go!"

The team hit the ground running, weapons raised, scanning for threats.

Tanner was the last one off, boots crunching against debris. The heat from smoldering wreckage radiated against his skin as he took in the sheer scale of destruction.

This wasn't just an attack.

This was a message.

\*\*\*

"Who the hell authorized your landing?"

The voice was sharp, cutting through the haze of smoke and tension.

Tanner turned toward the source, finding a tall, battle-worn figure storming toward them—Commander Julek. His scaled face was streaked with blood, one of his arms hastily bandaged, but his presence was still imposing.

Tanner barely had a second to introduce himself before Julek was on him.

"I don't have time to babysit off-worlders. You want to help? Then get back on your ship and get the hell out of my station."

Hale bristled, taking a step forward, but Tanner raised a hand to stop him.

"We're here to assist, Commander. You've got casualties. You've got a station hanging by a thread. We can help stabilize—"

"You think you're the first person to offer help?" Julek snapped. "You think we need more bodies getting in the way?"

His eyes flicked to the rest of the team, lingering for half a second too long on Alvarez and Mercer.

"You're soldiers. Soldiers kill things. What I need is engineers, power technicians, and infrastructure specialists. Do you have any of those with you?"

Tanner's jaw clenched.

"No, but—"

"Then you're in my way."

Behind him, a reactor console flickered erratically, sparks bursting from the cables that barely clung to the wall. The station was dying, and Julek was barely holding it together.

"We can at least secure your perimeter," Tanner tried.

"Too late for that." Julek's voice was cold, exhausted. "They already did what they came here to do."

Tanner gritted his teeth.

He wanted to argue, to stand his ground, but he knew a losing fight when he saw one. Julek didn't need soldiers. He needed a miracle.

And Tanner wasn't it.

"Fine." Tanner took a slow breath, reigning himself in. "But if you need us—"

"I won't."

Julek turned without another word, already barking orders at his remaining officers.

Tanner watched him go, frustration burning in his gut.

They had come to help.

Instead, they'd just wasted time.

***

Eagle Eight regrouped near the transport, waiting for orders.

"That was a waste," Mercer muttered. "We could've at least set up a perimeter."

"Doesn't matter," Alvarez said. "He wasn't going to let us."

Tanner was silent.

He hated this.

Hated feeling powerless.

Hated that he'd pulled his team into this mess when they should have been at the capital already.

Hale slung his rifle over his shoulder. "So, what now? Ambassador's waiting."

Tanner exhaled sharply.

"We move out."

As they boarded the transport, the station grew smaller behind them, its smoke still rising against the sky.

A symbol of failure.

And a reminder—

Tanner wasn't getting everything right.

And next time, someone might die because of it.

# CHAPTER 28

## A FRACTURED ALLIANCE

The transport touched down on the landing pad outside the capital's diplomatic sector, but the tension inside the cabin hadn't eased.

Tanner had been silent the entire flight.

The failure at the power station weighed on him— not just because Julek had dismissed them, but because he knew, deep down, he'd made the wrong call.

They should have come here first.

Now, he had to answer for it.

"Brace for impact," Hale muttered under his breath.

The moment the ramp lowered, two heavily armed guards stood waiting. Behind them, Ambassador Ladrinen.

Tanner barely had a second to step forward before the ambassador's furious gaze locked onto him.

"Lieutenant Tanner."

"Ambassador."

Ladrinen's tone was ice.

"So good of you to finally make time for me."

\*\*\*

The moment they were inside the diplomatic chamber, Ladrinen didn't hold back.

"Tell me, Lieutenant, what exactly was more important than my safety?"

Tanner squared his shoulders. "Sir, I assessed the situation and determined that the power station was—"

"The power station?" Ladrinen cut him off, his voice sharp. "You diverted to an infrastructure site instead of coming directly to your assigned post?"

Tanner clenched his jaw.

"That station is the lifeline of this city. If it fails, so does everything else."

Ladrinen leaned forward, his scaled hands pressing against the polished stone table between them.

"And what about my protection? Do you think the Mana faction will spare me because they damaged my power grid?"

"I didn't say that."

"But you acted like it."

The words landed like a strike.

Tanner said nothing.

"Do you think your war experience gives you the right to choose what matters here?" Ladrinen pressed. "You're not on Earth, Lieutenant. This is my world, and my people are the ones dying. Do you even understand that?"

Tanner felt his fists clench, but he forced his breathing to stay even.

"I understand that if the station falls, you'll have no defenses left."

"I don't need a lecture on logistics. I need a military unit that actually does its damn job."

The room fell into silence.

Tanner felt every eye on him.

And for the first time in a long while, he wasn't sure what to say.

\*\*\*

Ladrinen exhaled slowly, his anger shifting into something worse—disappointment.

"Tell me something, Lieutenant. If the Mana faction attacks again, and I am their target, will you be there to stop them? Or will you find another excuse to be elsewhere?"

Tanner didn't hesitate.

"I will be here."

Ladrinen studied him for a long moment, then slowly leaned back.

"You had better be."

Tanner nodded once, then turned on his heel and walked out, his team following behind.

***

The hallway felt colder than when they'd arrived.

Hale was the first to break the silence.

"That could've gone worse."

Tanner didn't reply.

Mercer shot him a look. "Sir?"

Tanner stopped, exhaling sharply.

I should have come here first.

I should have prioritized the ambassador.

I should have made the right call.

But he hadn't.

And now, everything was falling apart.

His team was doubting him.

His allies didn't trust him.

A thought hit Tanner like a punch to the gut.

Suzy.

- The reason he left home. The reason he enlisted.
- What if I never left? What if I had fought for her instead?
- Would I have been happier?

For the first time in a long time, he wasn't sure of the answer.

# CHAPTER 29

## A VOICE IN THE DARK

Lemma froze.

The faint crunch of rock under boots echoed above. More movement.

The patrol had returned.

Her pulse spiked, breath shallow as she pressed herself deeper into the crevice between the notched stone walls, her injured leg screaming in protest.

She clenched her jaw, biting back the pain. She couldn't let them hear her.

Stay still. Stay silent.

The dim light shifted, flickering along the cavern walls.

The search party was closer than before.

Her hands curled into fists. She wasn't sure how much longer she could stay hidden.

Then—

Her foot slipped.

***

Pain erupted as her bad leg gave out, her weight suddenly shifting.

Her shoulder slammed against the stone, and despite her best effort to hold it in—

A pained gasp escaped her lips.

She clamped a hand over her mouth, eyes wide in panic.

Had they heard?

The voices above halted.

Silence.

Lemma's heart pounded. She squeezed her eyes shut, trying to will the pain away, to stay still, to stay quiet.

Then—

A new sound.

Soft. Different.

A voice—familiar.

"Lemma? Are you there? Are you okay?"

Lemma's eyes shot open.

She knew that voice.

Park.

Relief surged through her, but it was immediately drowned out by pain as she tried to shift toward the sound.

"H-Here," she rasped, barely above a whisper.

Footsteps hurried closer, cautious but urgent.

Then, a silhouette appeared above the cavern entrance, framed against the dim glow of the patrol's torches flickering in the distance.

Erin Park.

Her sharp, watchful eyes scanned the cavern until they locked onto Lemma's form—bruised, bloodied, trapped.

Park hissed under her breath. "Damn it." She climbed down carefully, keeping her voice low.

"You look like hell."

Lemma managed a weak smirk despite the agony. "Feel worse."

Park knelt beside her, quickly assessing the injuries.

Leg—swollen, likely sprained or fractured.

Side—badly bruised, possibly broken ribs.

Breathing—labored.

She wasn't getting out of here on her own.

Park set a hand on Lemma's shoulder, her voice steady.

"Stay put. I'm going for help."

Lemma gritted her teeth, nodding weakly.

She had no choice but to trust her.

As Park disappeared back into the tunnels, Lemma exhaled a shaky breath, pressing herself against the cold stone.

She just had to hold on.

Help was coming.

# CHAPTER 30

## A RISKY RESCUE

Park moved swiftly through the tunnels, slipping through the shadows with practiced precision. Every few steps, she glanced back, ensuring she wasn't followed.

She had barely found Lemma in time—now she had to get back to the advance team before the Mana patrols doubled back.

After a tense, silent sprint, she reached the temporary hideout where Lemma's team had been waiting for clearance to begin their survey.

They weren't expecting her.

The moment she burst through the entrance, all eyes locked on her.

"What happened? Where's Lemma?" one of the operatives asked, stepping forward.

Park didn't waste time.

"She's injured. Trapped. Patrols are sweeping the area. We need to extract her—now."

The team muttered among themselves, but before anyone could react, one person pushed forward—Lieutenant Cooks.

A young but fiercely determined medic, Cooks had been on edge for days, waiting for orders to move.

"I need to get to her," Cooks insisted, eyes flashing with urgency. "If she's hurt, I can stabilize her before she gets worse. I have to go!"

Park hesitated. "We're calling in Eagle Eight. We move when they're in position."

Cooks' face darkened with frustration, but Park ignored it, reaching for her comm unit.

She needed to get a signal out.

She needed to call Tanner.

\*\*\*

Inside the capital, Tanner stood rigid, locked in a tense conversation with Ambassador Ladrinen.

The ambassador was still livid over Tanner's decision to divert to the power station, and it was taking every ounce of patience to keep the situation from unraveling further.

Then Mercer appeared at his side.

"Lieutenant. We need to talk. Now."

His voice was low, urgent.

Tanner barely spared him a glance. "Not now."

Mercer didn't back off. Instead, he grabbed Tanner's arm—firm but not aggressive—and leaned in.

"This isn't optional. Hallway. Now."

The tone made Tanner's stomach drop.

Without another word, he excused himself and followed Mercer into the hallway, shutting the door behind them.

The moment they were alone, Mercer turned to him, voice hushed but tense with urgency.

"I have Park on comms. She's found Lemma. She's injured and surrounded. We need to get to them right away."

Tanner stiffened.

"How bad?"

"No solid details, but Park says she's in rough shape. Can't move on her own. The medic with Lemma's team is begging to go stabilize her while we mobilize."

Tanner's mind raced.

It was too dangerous.

A lone medic rushing toward an injured asset in enemy territory?

It was a death sentence.

Tanner shook his head, decision firm.

"Deny the request. She holds position until we secure the site. Assemble the team. We move now."

Mercer nodded sharply, immediately relaying the command.

Tanner took a steadying breath, then turned back toward the ambassador's office.

Before he even reached the door, he stopped.

A sick feeling settled in his gut.

Was this the right call?

\*\*\*

Back at the advance team's hideout, Cooks' comm crackled.

"Stand fast. Do not proceed to Lemma's location. Eagle Eight is en route."

Cooks stared at the radio in disbelief.

Then anger took over.

"Are you kidding me?" she snapped. "She could be bleeding out, and we're just supposed to wait?!"

Park glared. "Those are our orders. We hold position. We can't risk another casualty."

Cooks wasn't listening.

She grabbed her medic bag and moved toward the tunnel entrance.

Park blocked her path.

"Cooks—"

"Move."

"You go in there, and you'll get yourself killed!"

Cooks locked eyes with Park, jaw clenched.

Then she did something Park didn't expect.

She grabbed Park's arm and yanked her forward.

"Then don't let me die alone."

Park cursed under her breath.

Before she could fully react, they were moving—rushing back through the dark tunnels toward Lemma.

Orders be damned.

They weren't leaving her behind.

# CHAPTER 31

## RACING AGAINST TIME

Park and Cooks moved quickly but carefully, sticking to the shadows of the cavern walls as they maneuvered through the winding tunnels. Torchlight flickered above, signaling the presence of Mana patrols still sweeping the area.

Cooks was breathing heavily, her medic bag bouncing against her hip as she followed Park's lead.

"Almost there," Park whispered. "Stay quiet. If we get spotted, this whole thing goes to hell."

Cooks didn't respond, her jaw clenched in determination.

Finally, they reached the hidden crevice where Lemma lay.

Park ducked inside first, sweeping the area before motioning for Cooks to follow.

Lemma was still there, her breathing ragged, eyes dull with pain.

The moment Cooks saw her, she rushed forward, already pulling supplies from her bag.

"Lie still, Lemma. I've got you."

Lemma gave a weak smirk, her voice barely above a whisper.

"Nice to see someone cares."

Cooks ignored the sarcasm and went straight to work, checking Lemma's vitals, scanning for internal injuries with a handheld diagnostic scanner.

Park, meanwhile, leaned against the cavern wall, muttering under her breath.

"I swear, if I have to keep running back and forth through these tunnels, I'm gonna lose my damn mind."

She turned toward Cooks and Lemma.

"Keep low, keep quiet. Do not move unless absolutely necessary."

Cooks nodded, barely looking up from her work.

"Just get the team here fast, or we'll all be screwed."

Park sighed sharply, then turned and slipped back into the tunnels, already dreading the trip back.

Somebody had to lead Eagle Eight in.

And that someone was her.

# CHAPTER 32

## INTO THE DEPTHS

Tanner kept his expression neutral, standing firm before Ambassador Ladrinen, who had made it clear—he wasn't happy.

The ambassador's reptilian gaze narrowed, his irritation palpable.

"Lieutenant Tanner, I have allowed you one mistake. You chose to divert to the power station instead of coming directly to me. Now, you wish to leave again?"

Tanner didn't hesitate. His voice was steady, professional, convincing.

"Your safety is our highest priority, Ambassador."

Ladrinen's eyes flicked over him, studying him carefully.

Tanner continued before the ambassador could interrupt.

"My team is going to reinforce the security perimeter. After last night's attack on the power station, we can't risk another blindside. If another assault comes, we need to be ready."

Ladrinen huffed, arms crossed.

"And yet, your forces will be beyond my walls. How does that protect me?"

Tanner gave a practiced nod, as if it were all part of the plan.

"We need to see what's out there before it gets to you. If an attack is forming, we need to detect it early."

A beat of silence.

Ladrinen finally sighed, pinching the bridge of his nose.

"Very well, Lieutenant. But do not let this become another diversion."

Tanner saluted sharply.

"Understood, sir. We'll return as soon as we confirm security."

Without waiting for more questions, Tanner turned and strode out, maintaining his calm, commanding pace until the doors sealed behind him.

Only then did he let out a slow exhale.

Mercer leaned in slightly, smirking.

"You are getting way too good at lying to politicians."

Tanner shot him a look.

"Let's move before he changes his mind."

***

Eagle Eight met up with Lemma's advance team, who were already on edge after Park and Cooks had run off.

Hale grunted, adjusting his rifle.

"So let me get this straight—we're heading into a cave system crawling with hostiles to extract an injured intel officer and a rogue medic and fight our way back out?"

Tanner locked his weapon into place.

"That about sums it up."

Mercer let out a low whistle.

"Sounds like a suicide mission."

Tanner shot him a look.

"Then it's a good thing we don't die easy."

Alvarez checked her gear, then nodded toward the cave entrance.

"We better move before the whole damn Mana faction figures out what's going on down there."

Without another word, Eagle Eight descended into the tunnels.

***

The first ambush came barely five minutes in.

A patrol of four Mana soldiers rounded a tight corridor just as Eagle Eight was moving through.

"Contact left!" Hale bellowed, opening fire.

The tight space erupted with gunfire, flashes of blue-white light illuminating the cavern in rapid bursts.

Tanner ducked behind a rock as Mercer dropped one of the hostiles with a single well-placed shot.

The enemy barely had a chance to react before Alvarez and Park flanked from the side, cutting them down in seconds.

"Clear!" Hale called, reloading.

Tanner didn't waste time.

"Move! We're on the clock!"

***

As they pressed deeper, the air grew thick and stale, the tunnels winding into a maze of forgotten history. Tanner's helmet-mounted light caught glimpses of ancient carvings along the walls—symbols and patterns that meant nothing to him but everything to Lemma.

Gunfire cracked again up ahead.

"That came from Lemma's position," Park said, voice tight.

Tanner gave the order immediately.

"Double-time it! Move!"

They pushed forward, weaving between rock formations, staying low as they closed the distance.

***

The next battle was fierce and fast.

A half-dozen Mana fighters had discovered Lemma's position, pinning down her and Cooks behind a natural rock alcove.

Cooks had dragged Lemma into cover, using her own body as a shield while she worked to keep her stable. A pistol clutched in her shaking hands, barely enough firepower to keep the enemy at bay.

Then Eagle Eight arrived like a thunderclap.

"Suppressing fire!"

Hale and Mercer lit up the cavern entrance, forcing the enemy to scatter.

Tanner rushed forward, sliding into cover beside Lemma and Cooks.

"You ladies order a rescue?"

Lemma let out a weak chuckle through the pain.

"About damn time."

Cooks glared at him.

"You could've let me come earlier!"

Tanner ignored her, already helping Lemma to her feet.

"Can you walk?"

Lemma's face twisted in pain, but she nodded.

"Not well."

"Good enough. Let's move."

***

With Hale and Alvarez leading the way, the team fought through two more quick skirmishes before finally reaching the cave entrance.

As they emerged into the open, the capital's skyline loomed in the distance, a reminder that they weren't out of the fire yet.

Tanner glanced at Lemma, then at Cooks.

"Next time, follow orders."

Cooks huffed, crossing her arms.

"Next time, don't make me break them."

Tanner started to reply but stopped.

For the first time, he really looked at her.

Cooks' face was still flushed from exertion, her hazel eyes sharp, and strands of long, red hair had come loose from her helmet, framing her face.

She was young but fiercely competent, and Tanner couldn't help but notice…

She was incredibly attractive.

That realization hit him harder than the last firefight.

Not the time, Tanner.

He shook it off, refocusing.

"Let's get the hell out of here."

Eagle Eight had secured their people.

But war was still coming.

# CHAPTER 33

## A QUIET MOMENT

Tanner navigated the winding halls of the temporary medical ward, his footsteps quiet against the polished floor.

The day had been a mess. His decisions had backfired, the ambassador didn't trust him, and Eagle Eight had been forced to retreat when they should have been making progress.

But right now, none of that mattered.

Right now, he needed to check on Lemma.

He turned the final corner and stepped inside the dimly lit medical bay, his gaze landing immediately on the cot in the far corner.

Lemma was there, propped up slightly, her face pale but alert. The deep bruising along her side and leg looked painful, but she was alive.

Sitting beside her, Lt. Cooks.

The medic was focused, checking Lemma's vitals, adjusting the medical bandages wrapped around her leg. A few loose strands of long red hair had slipped from her ponytail, framing her freckled face.

Tanner cleared his throat, and both women looked up.

"How's she doing?"

Lemma gave a weak smirk.

"I am still on this side of the dirt."

Cooks shot Lemma a mildly exasperated look before turning to Tanner.

"She needs rest, and she's lucky she didn't break more than she did. Her ribs took a hell of a hit."

"You're making me sound fragile," Lemma muttered.

"You fell into a cavern and got surrounded by enemy patrols," Cooks shot back. "You are fragile."

Tanner chuckled, shaking his head. "She's got a point."

Lemma just huffed, leaning back against her pillow.

"So, what's the damage outside?"

Tanner sighed, running a hand through his hair. "We're still trying to figure that out."

Lemma nodded slowly, wincing slightly.

"You look like hell, by the way."

Tanner smirked. "Good. Matches how I feel."

Cooks finished making her adjustments, closed her med kit, and stood up.

"She's stable for now, but I need to check on supplies."

Tanner stepped aside, but as she passed, he caught the briefest hint of something in her expression.

A flicker of amusement. Maybe something more.

"Try not to make any more stupid calls today, sir."

Tanner raised an eyebrow.

"Was that a dig at my leadership or just general life advice?"

Cooks smiled just enough for it to be noticeable.

"A little of both."

And just like that, she was gone.

Tanner watched her leave, something unsettlingly distracting about the way she carried herself—all confidence, no hesitation.

He turned back to Lemma, who was watching him closely.

A knowing smirk spread across her face.

"You're staring."

Tanner rolled his eyes. "I'm not staring."

"You totally are."

"You need more meds."

Lemma just laughed, shaking her head as Tanner sat down in the chair beside her.

For the first time in what felt like forever, the tension eased—just a little.

# CHAPTER 34

## PIECES OF THE PUZZLE

It had been a week since Lemma's rescue, and while the worst of her injuries had started to heal, she still moved with a stiffness she hated.

Resting in the med bay had been torture. She wasn't built for sitting still, not when she knew there were answers waiting to be uncovered.

That's why she was here, despite the lingering soreness in her ribs and the occasional hitch in her breath.

Dr. Elias Vance barely glanced up as she entered his research quarters, his sharp eyes locked on a digital tablet, scanning over newly processed data.

"You're supposed to be resting."

"I've rested enough." Lemma lowered herself into a chair, masking the discomfort as best she could.

Vance sighed, setting the tablet down.

"You and I have very different definitions of 'enough.'"

Lemma smirked. "And yet, here I am."

Vance didn't argue; they just studied her carefully before tapping the tablet screen.

"You risked a lot to bring this data back. Tell me, what do you think you found?"

Lemma straightened slightly, ignoring the pull of her ribs, and leaned forward. She tapped the screen, highlighting a repeating sequence of symbols.

"These markings appear multiple times, but with slight variations. They align with known shifts in the planet's sun phases. It's not just a historical record—it's an equation. They were tracking something."

Vance's analytical gaze narrowed, his mind already racing ahead.

"Tracking... or warning?"

Lemma exhaled slowly.

"I don't know yet. But the last recorded phase shift matches what's happening now."

"Which means they knew this was coming," Vance muttered. "And they left. The question is—why? Did they escape, or did they fail?"

Before Lemma could answer, the door slid open.

\*\*\*

Tanner stepped inside, his presence filling the room. He looked worn down but steady, his uniform still showing the wear of long shifts and little sleep.

Lemma hadn't seen much of him since the rescue, just a few check-ins and a nod here and there. But now, he was here—and she wasn't sure why.

"Bad time?"

Lemma smirked. "Always. Take a seat."

Tanner pulled up a chair beside her, his movements slower than usual. Whether it was exhaustion or something deeper, Lemma couldn't tell.

Vance glanced at him, then back at Lemma.

"Does he know science?"

"Not really," Lemma admitted.

Tanner scoffed, sitting up straighter.

"I have a master's in aerospace engineering and a minor in environmental engineering," he said, giving Vance a pointed look. "So, yeah. I know science."

Vance raised an eyebrow.

"And yet, you joined the military."

Tanner smirked. "And yet, here I am."

Lemma let out a soft chuckle, shaking her head.

"Alright, Einstein. Since you're here, try to keep up."

Tanner leaned forward, glancing at the sketched translations.

"So, best case, we figure out what happened to the last people who lived here. Worst case, we're reading their obituary."

"Pretty much," Lemma said.

"Great."

Tanner didn't have anything useful to add, but he stayed anyway.

Just being there.

And for Lemma, after everything, that was enough.

# CHAPTER 35

## TRAINING DAY

The afternoon sun hung low, casting long shadows across the training range as Eagle Eight prepped for drills. The air was thick with the clicks and snaps of weapons being checked, magazines being loaded, and gear being adjusted.

Tanner sat on an ammo crate, carefully loading rounds into a magazine, his movements deliberate but slow. His fingers were starting to ache from the repeated pressure of pressing each round down and sliding in the next.

Across from him, Hale was loading his own mags with practiced ease. His movements were fluid, efficient, and almost lazy.

Then he glanced up, noticing Tanner struggling.

With a smirk, he set his own gear down and walked over.

"Let me show you a trick I learned in the Navy."

Tanner looked up, raising an eyebrow.

Before he could respond, Park—seated nearby, checking her rifle—spoke up.

"Salty, you were never in the Navy."

Hale just grinned and winked. "Details."

Ignoring her, he crouched next to Tanner and took one of the spare magazines.

"You're fighting the spring too much," Hale said, positioning the mag in Tanner's hand. "Use your thumb to push down on the last round before you slide the next one in. Less resistance, easier on the fingers."

He demonstrated, loading a round effortlessly before handing the mag back.

Tanner gave it a try, and sure enough, it was smoother. Faster.

He let out a small chuckle, shaking his head.

"Thanks. 'Salty Dog,' huh? One of these days, you'll have to tell me the story on how you got that name."

Hale flashed a knowing smirk as he grabbed another magazine.

"Yeah, sure. Another time."

Tanner didn't push.

But he filed that away for later.

*\*\*\**

Just as Tanner was about to load another mag, movement caught his eye.

Cooks walked past, her long red hair pulled into a loose ponytail, a med kit slung over her shoulder. Even in the rough setting of the training yard, there was something effortlessly confident about her.

Tanner's gaze lingered.

A little too long.

Suddenly, Park's hand shot out, backhanding him on the shoulder.

"Stare much?"

Tanner jerked slightly, blinking as if caught red-handed.

"I wasn't—"

Park just gave him a deadpan look.

"Uh-huh."

Hale, without looking up, added casually, "Careful LT., Medics have a way of making you regret poor life choices."

Before Tanner could come up with a response, Maddox, overhearing the exchange, leaned in with a wide grin.

"Oh yeah, you better be careful, boss. Medics are dangerous. One minute they're patching you up; the next, they're sewing your ass to a cot so you actually rest."

Hale snorted. "That happen to you, Maddox?"

"I don't wanna talk about it."

Tanner shook his head, exhaling as he picked up another magazine.

This time, with a slight smirk on his face.

# CHAPTER 36

## UNWANTED DUTY

The moment they landed, Ladrinen was furious.

"This was a complete overreaction."

Tanner stepped off the ramp, fighting the urge to roll his eyes. "A situation was developing, and I acted on it."

"You embarrassed me! There was no real threat!"

"And if I was wrong, we're alive. If I was right, we're still alive."

Ladrinen's tail flicked in irritation.

"Unacceptable. You will need to explain yourself, Lieutenant."

Tanner didn't respond. The ambassador stormed off, leaving Eagle Eight to disembark from the transport.

Tanner exhaled, finally feeling the strain in his ankle.

It hurt.

But he wasn't about to let anyone—

"You're limping."

Tanner turned his head to see Cooks standing at the edge of the ramp, arms crossed.

"I'm fine."

Cooks wasn't buying it.

"Uh-huh." She stepped closer, eyes narrowing. "You rolled your ankle, didn't you?"

"I'm fine."

"You keep saying that, and yet, I keep noticing the limp."

Tanner sighed, running a hand over his face.

"It's nothing."

"Sure, and I'm a five-star chef."

Before he could protest, she grabbed his arm, pulling him toward the medical tent.

"Cooks, I really don't—"

"Shut up and come with me, LT."

As she led him off, Tanner tried—and failed—not to notice the way her hair caught in the sunlight or the slight smirk playing on her lips.

Park, passing by, saw the whole thing.

She smirked before calling out:

"Stare much?"

Tanner sighed. "Not a damn word, Park."

She just grinned.

Inside the medical tent, Cooks had Tanner seated on the exam table, already working efficiently.

"Boot off, LT. Let's see how bad you messed this up."

Tanner huffed but didn't argue, unzipping and pulling off the boot with a grimace as his ankle throbbed in protest.

Cooks crouched down, carefully rolling his sock away and lightly pressing against the swollen joint.

"Well, congrats, you didn't completely wreck it. Probably a mild sprain. Some rest, ice, and not being an idiot for a few days, and you'll be fine."

Tanner scoffed. "Not being an idiot? I don't know if I can make that promise."

Cooks grinned. "Yeah, I figured."

She grabbed the diagnostic scanner from the table and switched it on. "Gotta check your vitals while you're here, standard procedure."**

Tanner didn't argue, letting her work. She clipped the pulse monitor onto his finger and started the scan.

As the screen displayed his heart rate, her brow furrowed slightly.

His pulse was elevated.

Her eyes flicked to his ankle, then back to the readings.

This injury wouldn't cause an elevated heart rate.

She looked up just in time to see a faint red tinge on his cheeks.

With an inward sigh, she was starting to get the idea.

Trying to suppress a smirk, she tapped his shoulder playfully, grinning.

"You okay there, LT.?"

Tanner blinked. "What?"

Cooks tilted her head. "You sure your heart rate is from the injury and not... something else?"

Tanner opened his mouth—then closed it.

"...I'm fine."

Cooks chuckled. "Uh-huh. That's what I thought."

She finished up her scan, rolling her eyes playfully. "Alright, hotshot. You'll live. Try not to roll it again, or I'm keeping you in here longer just to annoy you."

Tanner smirked. "Now I'm tempted just to see what happens."

Cooks raised an eyebrow. "Don't test me, LT."

With that, she patted his good leg and stood up, already putting her equipment away.

Tanner exhaled, forcing himself not to overthink whatever that was.

He slid his boot back on, testing the weight on his ankle.

Still sore, but nothing he couldn't push through.

As he stood, Cooks gave him a final glance, eyes still dancing with amusement.

"Try not to do anything stupid for at least twenty-four hours, alright?"

"No promises," Tanner said with a grin.

She just shook her head, muttering something about "reckless officers" before heading off.

Tanner watched her go a little longer than necessary before sighing and stepping outside.

Where Park was waiting.

Arms crossed. Smirking.

"Stare much?"

Tanner groaned. "For the last time, Park—"

"Yeah, yeah, 'not a damn word.'" She grinned. "You make this too easy."

Tanner shook his head, limping off with zero intention of discussing this further.

Somehow, despite the pain, the day suddenly didn't feel quite as bad.

# CHAPTER 37

## THE RACE FOR ANSWERS

Lemma paced the length of the research lab, the dim light of the holo-table casting shifting symbols against her face. Her fingers clenched and unclenched at her sides as she stared at the translated glyphs floating before her.

It wasn't enough.

Not even close.

For days, she had worked through the markings retrieved from the archives—cross-referencing patterns, comparing them to Earth-based languages, looking for any missing piece that would explain what these ancient people were trying to say.

But the answers weren't here.

They were still down there—in the caves.

"How the hell does this tie to Christianity?" Lemma muttered, pressing her fingers to her temples. "What are they trying to tell us about the sun?"

She had the warnings—phrases carved into the stone, referencing a coming storm, a time of reckoning, some kind of 'Veil of Protection'.

But was it science? A prophecy? Both?

They left these messages for a reason. We just don't understand them yet.

A sigh from across the table pulled her out of her spiral.

"Running yourself in circles again?"

She looked up to find Dr. Vance rubbing his eyes, pushing his glasses up onto his forehead as he scrolled through a mess of calculations.

"I don't have the luxury of waiting," she shot back. "We need answers."

"And I need a miracle," Vance replied dryly. "So I guess we're both out of luck."

Lemma exhaled sharply, forcing herself to calm down.

"How bad is it?"

Vance leaned back in his chair, gesturing to the projections on his screen.

"Bad."

"How bad?"

"Civilization-ending bad."

The weight of his words settled like iron in her chest.

"We don't have the tech to stop the sun from destabilizing," Vance continued. "If we don't find a way to shield the cities, we're looking at mass casualties in weeks."

Lemma closed her eyes, the weight of it all pressing against her.

"Then we go back," she said, opening them again. "We fight our way back into the cave and retrieve the rest of the tablets."

Vance gave her a long look, then sighed.

"Tanner's not gonna like that."

\*\*\*

Tanner did not, in fact, like that.

"You want us to go back into the same cave system that nearly got you killed?"

He stood at the head of the mission table, arms braced against the table, his frustration barely restrained. The rest of Eagle Eight was gathered, listening intently.

"We don't have a choice," Lemma countered. "I don't have enough information to decode the warnings. Without it, we can't stop what's coming."

Tanner exhaled sharply, turning toward Vance.

"And you? Still no luck on your end?"

Vance shook his head.

"We need a shielding system capable of filtering out dangerous solar radiation while still allowing energy to pass through. Right now? We don't have the power or the tech to make that happen."

Tanner rubbed a hand down his face.

"So, let me get this straight—we need to go back into a fortified cave system swarming with enemy forces to retrieve stone tablets that might tell us how to fix all of this?"

"Yes," Lemma and Vance said at the same time.

Tanner sighed.

"Why is it never easy?"

\*\*\*

As the team began prepping their gear, Tanner double-checked his rifle's sights, his mind still processing everything.

He felt Cooks approaching before she even spoke.

"You good, LT.?"

He glanced up.

She was leaning against the supply table, arms crossed, watching him with that same half-smirk she always had when she knew something was bugging him.

"I'll be better when we have a plan that doesn't involve running straight into enemy fire," Tanner muttered.

Cooks snorted. "Yeah, well... that's kind of your thing, isn't it?"

Tanner shook his head but couldn't hide his smirk.

Cooks tapped his shoulder playfully. "You'll probably figure it out."

He met her eyes—for just a second too long.

Cooks must have noticed because her smirk softened just slightly before she turned back toward the supply crates.

Get your head in the game, Tanner.

He exhaled, shaking it off, and called out to the team.

"Alright, listen up! We're going back in. We do this fast, we do this clean, and we get the hell out. Wheels up in twenty."

Eagle Eight moved out.

The race for answers had begun.

# CHAPTER 38

## THE RISING THREAT

Tanner barely had time to breathe before the next problem hit.

The reports started coming in early in the morning, right as the team was wrapping up their gear check for the upcoming cave assault.

"Multiple breaches along the outer city defenses."

"Power station is running on emergency reserves."

"Increased movement from Mana faction cells—suspected sabotage teams in play."

Tanner gritted his teeth, scrolling through the latest security feed updates on his datapad. The entire region was heating up and fast.

Eagle Eight had barely stabilized the last situation, and now things were getting worse.

***

"This is unacceptable!"

Ambassador Ladrinen's voice echoed across the chamber, his sharp, reptilian features twisting with barely controlled frustration.

Tanner stood across from him, arms folded, waiting for the rant to end.

"The Mana faction is emboldened! They strike at our power grid, our infrastructure, and now—now they breach the city's perimeter? Where is your so-called elite team in all of this, Lieutenant?"

Tanner kept his expression neutral. "Stopping this is exactly what we're working on, sir."

"Then work faster."

Tanner exhaled, reigning in his temper.

"If we go in blind, we'll lose more than time. We need those archive tablets to understand what's happening with the sun—"

"Damn your tablets!" Ladrinen snapped. "We need soldiers in the streets, securing the city! What good is stopping the sun if we're all dead before it even reaches us?"

Tanner knew the ambassador had a point.

They weren't just fighting the sun's instability— they were fighting to keep the planet from tearing itself apart before it even got to that point.

This whole thing is unraveling faster than we can hold it together.

But that didn't change the mission.

\*\*\*

Tanner found Lemma and Dr. Vance in the research sector, surrounded by a sea of glowing screens and ancient stone slabs.

Vance barely looked up from his data.

"You're back faster than I expected. Good news?"

"If you consider the entire city about to become a battlefield 'good news,' then sure."

Vance finally looked up, rubbing tiredly at his temples.

"That tracks. We're out of time either way."

Tanner frowned. "You're saying it's happening sooner?"

Lemma stood, rubbing her shoulder as she exhaled. "We can't be sure, but from everything we've translated so far, this isn't a slow decline—it's a breaking point. Once the sun reaches the next phase shift, things are going to get exponentially worse."

Vance nodded. "At this rate, we're looking at days, maybe a week, before the radiation levels become lethal for unshielded zones."

Days?

Tanner let that sink in.

***

"So what are we looking at?" Tanner asked, scanning the display. "How do we stop this?"

Vance ran a frustrated hand through his graying hair.

"We can't stop it. We can only try to protect what's left."

"And that's not working either," Lemma muttered, leaning against the table. "Everything we've tried—every shielding model Vance has run—fails under direct solar impact."

Tanner's jaw clenched.

"There's got to be a way."

Vance sighed, shaking his head. "Not with the tech we have."

***

Before they could argue further, Tanner's comm crackled.

"LT, you're gonna want to get down here."

It was Mercer, his voice tense.

"What is it?"

"The power station. We just lost another generator. The next failure, and we're looking at a complete collapse."

# CHAPTER 39

## FIGHTING BACK TO THE CAVES

Tanner stood near the open cargo bay of the dropship, his gaze locked on the dusty expanse of terrain stretching toward the cave entrance. The battle had already started.

From above, he could see the flashes of weapons fire illuminating the cavern's outer defenses—Mana faction forces had dug in, turning the entrance into a kill zone.

This is gonna be messy.

Behind him, Eagle Eight was gearing up.

Park double-checked her rifle, preparing to clear a path through enemy snipers.

Hale loaded up heavy rounds, muttering about how much he hated "digging out rats."

Mercer prepped the comms scrambler, ensuring the enemy couldn't call in reinforcements too soon.

Cooks tightened her medical pack, her eyes flicking toward Tanner just long enough for him to notice.

"You better not need me out there, LT."

Tanner smirked. "I'll try my best."

No promises.

\*\*\*

The dropship came in fast and low, kicking up a storm of dust and smoke as the side doors slid open.

"Go! Go! Go!"

Tanner hit the ground first, rolling into cover behind a half-collapsed structure as enemy fire rained down.

"Contact on the ridge!" Park called, already sighting her rifle.

A sharp crack echoed through the canyon as she took down the first sniper.

Hale unleashed hell, his rounds tearing through an enemy emplacement as Eagle Eight pushed forward.

Tanner's boots hit the rock, pushing through the dust as he sprinted toward the cave entrance.

"Alvarez, take left! Mercer, get that jammer online!"

Explosions rocked the ridge, sending debris cascading down as Tanner fired two quick shots, dropping a pair of Mana soldiers before they could reposition.

"LT, we're clear to move in!"

Tanner signaled for the team to advance, their weapons up as they disappeared into the darkness of the cave system.

***

Inside, the air was thick with dust and tension. The narrow corridors forced them into tight formations, and the flickering lights from ancient sconces barely illuminated the twisting tunnels ahead.

"Keep it quiet," Tanner murmured. "Park, take point."

They moved deeper, weapons up, senses sharp.

Then, a noise—too soft for normal conversation, but there.

"Hold," Tanner whispered.

Park pressed against the stone wall, peering around a bend.

"Four targets. Setting up a barricade."

"We can't let them reinforce."

Tanner motioned silently—they were going in hard and fast.

With precision, they struck.

Park dropped the first before they even saw her.

Hale took the second with a brutal short burst.

Tanner moved in, knocking the third unconscious before he could raise the alarm.

Mercer jammed enemy comms as they secured the area.

"We're getting close," Lemma said, scanning the cave walls. "The archive chamber should be ahead."

But as she took another step, the ground trembled.

Then came the roar of reinforcements.

\*\*\*

Mana forces came from both sides, cutting off their retreat.

"Ambush!"

Gunfire exploded in the confined space.

Tanner dove behind cover, his rifle kicking as he returned fire.

"We need to get inside the archive!" Lemma called, pressing herself against a pillar for cover.

Cooks rushed to tend to a wounded soldier, barely dodging a near-miss from a plasma round.

Tanner gritted his teeth.

We're not getting pinned down here.

"Alvarez, grenade!"

Alvarez launched an explosive down the corridor, the blast forcing the enemy to scatter.

That was their chance.

"Move! Now!"

Eagle Eight pushed forward, bullets and energy fire ripping past them as they made their way to the main archive chamber.

\*\*\*

They breached the chamber, weapons ready.

Breathing hard, Tanner scanned the room.

"Park, Mercer—cover the entrance. We're not getting boxed in again."

The two nodded, moving swiftly back toward the entrance to set up a defensive position.

Massive stone carvings lined the walls, glowing softly with unknown energy. The room hummed as if something ancient was waking up.

Lemma stepped forward, running her fingers over the engravings.

"This is it."

Tanner exhaled, lowering his rifle.

They had made it.

Now, they just had to figure out what the hell the ancients were trying to tell them.

Tanner turned to Lemma, his voice steady.

"We need to grab what we can and get out."

# CHAPTER 40

## THE LOST KNOWLEDGE

Tanner's pulse was still steady from the fight, but his focus was shifting fast. They weren't done yet—not even close.

"We need to grab what we can and get out," he repeated, scanning the chamber for threats.

Lemma barely heard him.

She stood frozen in place, her fingers tracing the engraved patterns on the massive stone walls as if she could pull meaning from them by touch alone. The markings glowed faintly, pulsing as if alive.

This was it.

Everything they needed to understand the sun's phase shift, the warnings left behind, the so-called 'Veil of Protection.'

And it's all here, staring me in the face.

But there was no time for slow decoding.

She needed to think fast.

\*\*\*

"LT, we've got movement outside," Park's voice cut through the tension, sharp and alert.

Tanner turned, catching her peering down the entrance corridor, her rifle tight against her shoulder.

"How many?"

"Too many."

Mercer's voice was grim. He was already working on setting up interference, jamming enemy comms to buy them a few more minutes.

"They're regrouping," Mercer added. "We don't have long before they make another push."

Tanner turned back to Lemma, voice firm.

"The Mana faction looks to be gearing up to come at us full force. Grab as many tablets as you can carry and let's go, Lemma."

Lemma hesitated for just a second, eyes scanning the walls, the engravings, the untouched knowledge that they were about to leave behind.

We don't have a choice.

With a tight jaw, she forced herself into action, pulling the most critical stone tablets from the central altar, stacking them carefully in her satchel.

Tanner motioned to Alvarez and Maddox to help grab as many as they could.

"Move fast. We don't need everything, just the key pieces."

Hale stood near the door, gripping his weapon tightly.

"LT, I really don't want to fight another damn battle in a cave."

Tanner shot him a pointed look.

"Then let's make sure we don't have to."

\*\*\*

With the last tablet secured, Tanner turned to Park and Mercer.

"Time's up. Fall back—now."

They moved fast, weaving back through the tunnels, keeping low and quiet as they pushed toward the exit.

"Alvarez, take rear guard. Maddox, you're on point with me."

The distant sound of footsteps echoed through the cavern, closing in from the passageways behind them.

"We don't have long before they find us," Mercer warned.

Tanner exhaled sharply, adjusting his grip on his rifle.

We're not getting pinned down again.

"Then we don't stop moving."

But just as they rounded a bend in the tunnel, the first volley of enemy fire slammed into the walls around them.

"Contact!" Park shouted.

A squad of Mana fighters had moved in, setting up a kill zone at the only exit.

"Push forward!" Tanner ordered, returning fire as they moved.

The tight corridors turned the fight into a brutal, close-quarters engagement. Bullets and energy rounds ripped through the darkness, sparking off the stone walls.

Alvarez took down two enemies with precise bursts, while Hale unloaded heavy rounds into the makeshift barricade ahead.

Maddox was right beside Tanner, laughing despite the chaos.

"Of all the ways to go, I swear you always pick the fun ones, LT!"

Tanner smirked despite himself, shoving forward through the hail of gunfire.

They were almost through.

Then Maddox staggered.

A sharp crack echoed through the tunnel, followed by a sickening thud as he hit the cavern floor.

"Maddox!" Cooks was already moving toward him, dropping beside him as Tanner and Alvarez covered her.

Maddox grunted, pressing his hand to his stomach, where blood was already pooling beneath his fingers.

"Shit..." His voice was weak, his usual humor fading.

Cooks worked fast, her hands moving with practiced precision, but her expression was tight.

Tanner knelt beside him. "You're gonna be fine, Maddox."

Maddox grinned weakly, shaking his head.

"Nah, LT... I think this is my stop."

Tanner's jaw clenched. "Not on my watch."

"Not up to you." Maddox's grip tightened briefly on Tanner's arm. "Get 'em out of here. Finish the job."

Cooks looked up, her expression grim. "He's losing too much blood."

More gunfire erupted down the tunnel.

"We have to move!" Park called.

Tanner forced himself to make the call.

He grabbed Maddox's hand, gripping it tight before pulling away.

"Hale, Mercer—carry him."

Hale's face hardened, and Mercer gave a quick nod before both men moved fast, lifting Maddox's limp body between them.

Cooks exhaled sharply, wiping the blood from her hands as she pushed herself up, her jaw tight with grief.

"Let's go," Tanner said, voice steel.

The moment they hit the next tunnel, enemy reinforcements swarmed in, forcing them into another vicious firefight.

"Cover Hale and Mercer!" Tanner barked, emptying another magazine as the team fought its way through.

With one final push, they burst into the open daylight, the cold air rushing over them like a slap to the face.

Their extraction dropship hovered above, ramp already lowered.

"Move, move, move!"

They piled in, rounds still flying past them as the doors slammed shut behind them.

The ship lifted off.

Tanner stood near the entrance, watching the cavern shrink beneath them.

They Maddox.

But they had made it.

And the fight wasn't over yet.

# CHAPTER 41

## THE SCIENTIFIC HURDLE

The ride back to base was somber, the usual post-mission debrief replaced with silence.

Tanner stood near the cargo bay doors, his knuckles white as he gripped the overhead railing. Across from him, Hale and Mercer sat on either side of Maddox's still form, neither speaking.

Cooks had tried, moving between them, checking for any last sign of life, but they all knew.

Maddox was gone.

They had pulled him out, but that didn't feel like a victory.

Lemma sat toward the front of the ship, hunched over the stone tablets in her lap, avoiding everyone's eyes. She was working, but Tanner could tell—she felt it too.

The price they'd paid.

He cracked jokes up until the end. Damn it, Maddox.

Tanner exhaled sharply, forcing his mind forward.

They still had a mission to finish.

***

The moment they landed, Vance was waiting.

Tanner barely had time to step off the ship before the scientist rushed forward, already scanning the recovered tablets.

"Did you get everything?"

"We got enough," Tanner said, his voice flat.

Vance barely registered the tension in the team, too caught up in the rush of new information.

Lemma stepped forward, handing him the most critical tablets.

"The ancients knew this phase shift was coming," she said. "They tried to counteract it, but their methods failed."

Vance's expression darkened as he turned toward the research sector.

"Then we better learn from their mistakes."

***

Hours later, the command center's research wing was filled with the sound of clacking keyboards and frustrated sighs.

The sun's radiation output was increasing, and the planet's energy infrastructure was collapsing.

Vance had mapped out a dozen different shielding models, each designed to protect the cities from the worst of the exposure.

Every single one failed.

Tanner stood with his arms crossed, watching the latest simulation crumble on-screen.

"So, what's the problem?"

Vance ran a hand through his graying hair, exhausted.

"The energy requirements are too damn high. Even if we had a perfect shielding model, there's no power grid on this planet strong enough to sustain it for more than a few hours."

Lemma sat nearby, flipping through translated inscriptions, her expression tightening.

"The ancients tried something similar," she muttered. "They referenced a 'Veil of Protection'—some kind of energy barrier designed to let in vital light but block the deadly radiation. It should have worked."

"But it didn't." Vance's voice was sharp. "Because they hit the same wall we just did. It's impossible at this scale."

Tanner exhaled, rubbing his temple.

"There's gotta be another angle. Some kind of workaround."

"We're out of angles," Vance snapped. "This is physics, Lieutenant. Not a damn strategy game."

\*\*\*

Tanner stayed quiet for a long moment, his mind pulling pieces together.

The shielding system needed to be sustainable. Self-regulating. Adaptable.

Like a living organism.

His gaze flicked toward the holo-display, watching as another failed shield model flickered out.

Then, suddenly, a memory resurfaced.

A project from years ago. College research he had written off as theoretical.

He straightened.

"What about a self-repairing structure?"

Vance frowned. "What?"

Tanner turned toward Mercer. "Pull up the molecular lattice structure of the last failed test. Now overlay it with dynamic self-assembling nanostructures—like microbial colonies."

Vance's brow furrowed, but he followed the logic.

Mercer worked fast, inputting the requested model.

The screen flickered.

Then, instead of collapsing under strain, the simulated structure shifted and adapted, reinforcing itself.

The team fell silent.

Vance stepped closer, his eyes scanning the data.

"Wait a minute… are you saying—"

Tanner nodded. "If we create an electromagnetic shielding mesh using tunable nano-particles, we don't have to power it constantly. It would regulate itself, expanding and contracting only when needed."

Lemma's eyes widened.

"That's the Veil of Protection."

Vance hesitated.

"This… might actually work."

For the first time since they'd landed, there was hope.

But they weren't there yet.

Tanner exhaled, steeling himself.

"Then let's get to work."

# CHAPTER 42

## THE SHIELDING CONCEPT

The command center's research lab was a flurry of movement. Screens glowed with real-time data streams, holo-displays projected shielding schematics, and in the middle of it all, Tanner, Lemma, Vance, and Mercer worked against time.

The model they had pieced together—the tunable electromagnetic nano-particle mesh—was still theoretical.

But it was the only viable solution.

The Veil of Protection wasn't just ancient mythology. It was a system—one that should have worked, if only they had the technology to sustain it.

Now, they did.

\*\*\*

Vance gestured to the massive holo-projection of the shield model, pacing as he spoke.

"If we make this work, the shield will be able to dynamically filter solar radiation, adjusting in real-time to only block the most harmful wavelengths."

Mercer, typing rapidly at the control panel, nodded without looking up.

"And because it's a self-regulating system, we won't need to draw continuous power—just enough to keep the nano-particles in alignment."

Lemma leaned forward, scanning the translated inscriptions they had retrieved from the cave.

"This is exactly what the ancients were trying to do."

Tanner, standing with arms crossed, watched the simulation run. The model held—but only under controlled conditions.

"What's the catch?" he asked, eyeing Vance.

The scientist sighed, rubbing his forehead.

"The catch is that we don't have time for a full-scale test. If this fails, the shield could collapse, frying everything underneath it."

Tanner nodded slowly. "So no pressure."

\*\*\*

We can expand "The Test Run" by adding more tension, making the experiment feel more uncertain, and emphasizing the risk involved. Instead of just saying, "It worked," we can describe how the shield reacts dynamically to the burst, nearly failing before adapting. This will build suspense and reinforce the stakes.

For "Preparing for Deployment," we can expand on the challenges of manufacturing the shield at scale, introduce logistical hurdles, and emphasize that this isn't just a plug-and-play solution—they'll need to work against time and deal with political pressure from the ambassador.

***

"Let's run a small-scale test."

Vance hesitated, tapping the control panel. "If this goes wrong, we could overload the containment field. Best case, the simulation collapses. Worst case... we blow half the lab."

Tanner exhaled sharply. "Not the kind of pep talk I was hoping for, Doc."

Mercer flicked through the settings on the control panel, locking in the parameters.

"Shield containment online. Setting nano-mesh to auto-adjust frequency."

The chamber hummed to life, the projected mesh shimmering into existence. It was barely visible, a faint distortion in the air.

Lemma stood close to the monitor, watching intently.

"Activating the pulse in three... two... one."

The system flared with energy. The artificial solar burst slammed into the shield.

For a split second, the entire model collapsed inward, shrinking as if about to rupture.

It's going to fail.

Tanner gritted his teeth, waiting for the system to collapse.

Then—the particles adjusted.

The mesh fluctuated, shifting dynamically, recalibrating to match the energy signature of the burst. The moment stretched, tension thick in the air—

And then, just as suddenly, the system stabilized.

The field held.

"Holy shit."

Mercer's voice broke the silence as the system displayed the final energy absorption data.

Vance exhaled sharply, his hands braced on the console.

"It... it worked."

Tanner shot him a look. "Not the most reassuring tone, Doc."

Vance straightened, still scanning the results.

"Because we don't know if it will scale up."

Lemma's eyes stayed locked on the holograms. "The ancients tried this on a much larger scale—and failed."

That killed the moment.

Tanner exhaled, rolling his shoulders. "So, we learn from their mistakes."

"And pray we don't repeat them," Lemma muttered.

***

Tanner turned to Mercer.

"How fast can we manufacture enough of this mesh to cover the cities?"

Mercer's fingers flew over the control panel, running calculations. The holo-screen displayed production estimates, material requirements, and energy consumption rates.

"If we get full access to the planetary energy refineries and all available production lines?" He paused, exhaling. "Maybe forty-eight hours. But that's assuming no resistance from the locals."

Tanner's expression darkened.

"The ambassador is going to fight us on this, isn't he?"

Vance let out a low, exhausted laugh. "Of course he is. The shielding concept goes against everything their government believes. Their people are still split between fighting this and thinking it's divine will."

Damn it.

Tanner ran a hand through his hair, thinking. "Alright. Then we convince them."

Lemma looked at him sharply. "And if they still refuse?"

Tanner's jaw tightened. "Then we do it anyway."

Vance sighed. "Diplomatic nightmare incoming."

"We don't have time for diplomacy. We have time for survival."

Tanner straightened.

"We move out in two hours. Get the plan locked in. We're making this happen."

Because if they didn't—

There wouldn't be anything left to save.

# CHAPTER 43

## PROOF OF CONCEPT

Tanner stood in the center of the war room, his arms crossed as the holographic shield model flickered above the table. The tension in the air was thick, and the faces around him weren't exactly receptive.

Across from him, Ambassador Ladrinen sat with a calculating expression, his reptilian eyes narrowed in deep thought. Beside him, Commander Julek looked visibly tense, his posture rigid, arms crossed over his chest.

Tanner had expected resistance.

What he hadn't expected was the absolute silence that followed Mercer's technical breakdown of the shield.

Great. They're either stunned by the brilliance of it or completely against it.

Finally, Ladrinen leaned forward, his yellow eyes gleaming under the dim war room lights.

"You want to construct a planetary-scale barrier around our cities... using self-replicating nano-particles?"

"That's the idea," Tanner said evenly.

Ladrinen exhaled through his nostrils, his clawed fingers tapping slowly against the table.

"You must understand my position, Lieutenant," he said, his voice smooth but carrying the weight of authority. "This proposal—if we accept it—will shape the future of my people. And you are asking me to put my trust in a human-made concept based on the failed designs of a civilization that no longer exists."

Tanner didn't flinch. "It's not the same design. We've improved it."

Ladrinen glanced at Dr. Vance, who stood beside Tanner, arms folded, waiting for his turn to speak.

"You assume your modifications will work. But if you're wrong, we lose everything."

Vance cleared his throat. "Ambassador, if we don't implement this, you'll lose everything anyway."

Ladrinen's gaze flicked toward him.

"Explain."

Vance gestured to the holo-projection, bringing up new energy readings.

"We've already recorded a twenty-percent increase in solar radiation reaching the surface. Based on what we now know from the ancient records, we're looking at a full planetary sterilization event within weeks."

"Your energy grids are already failing," Mercer added, leaning against the table. "If we don't get this system operational, even your underground shelters won't be enough."

Julek shifted, his clawed hands tightening into fists.

"That's if we can even get the shield powered in the first place."

Tanner turned toward him, finally getting to the real roadblock.

***

"You're worried about the grid."

Julek let out a harsh exhale, shaking his head.

"We barely have enough power to keep our current defenses online. The last Mana attack crippled the outer generators, and our reserves are running on backup systems."

Tanner nodded. "We anticipated that."

Mercer flipped the projection, revealing a secondary plan overlay.

"We only need localized nodes to get the shielding active. Once the first phase is up, the shield can self-sustain in cycles, drawing power only when necessary."

Ladrinen's eyes narrowed. "And how much will this first phase cost us?"

Mercer hesitated. "Significant resources."

Julek let out a low growl. "Then it's a moot point. We don't have enough reserves."

Tanner leaned forward, planting his hands on the table.

"Then we make more."

Julek scowled. "What, you think we can just fabricate energy?"

Tanner pointed to the planetary schematics on the projection.

"Not fabricate. Redirect. Your main geothermal plant is running at half-capacity due to the damaged substations, right?"

Julek hesitated, his jaw tightening. "Yes."

"Then we repair them."

The room fell into silence.

Ladrinen leaned back in his chair, studying Tanner carefully.

"You would commit your forces to securing our power grid? When you could simply force this plan through without our approval?"

Tanner didn't hesitate. "We're not here to rule your people. We're here to save them."

Julek let out a slow breath, shaking his head.

"It won't be easy. The Mana faction still controls three of the outer substations."

"Then we take them back."

***

Ladrinen exhaled, tapping his claws on the table once more.

"Let's say I agree. If we restore the power stations and stabilize the energy grid, how long will it take before we know if your shielding technology will work?"

Vance and Mercer exchanged glances.

"Once the first nodes are active? We'll know within hours."

Tanner let the moment stretch, watching Ladrinen carefully.

The ambassador closed his eyes briefly, considering. Then, with a slow nod, he finally spoke.

"You have your authorization."

Tanner didn't let out a breath of relief, not yet.

Ladrinen's gaze sharpened.

"But if this fails, Lieutenant…"

He let the implication hang.

Tanner held his gaze. "It won't."

Ladrinen exhaled and turned to Julek. "Make the necessary preparations."

Julek nodded stiffly.

Tanner straightened, locking eyes with his team.

"We move at dawn."

The hardest fight was still ahead of them.

# CHAPTER 44

## THE FINAL BATTLE

Tanner stood at the edge of the makeshift command center, watching the horizon burn red with the rising sun.

It wouldn't be long now.

The Mana faction knew what was coming. They had seen the construction efforts of the shielding nodes, the repairs to the power grid, and the gradual shift of control slipping from their grasp.

This was it.

Either they stopped the shield from coming online, or they would lose their ability to weaponize the chaos of the sun's phase shift.

They won't let that happen without a fight.

Tanner turned back to his team, gathered around a holo-table inside the operations tent.

Mercer was running last-minute system diagnostics, ensuring the shield nodes were ready for activation.

Hale was loading up extra ammunition, triple-checking his gear with a quiet intensity.

Alvarez was working with local forces, coordinating defensive positions around the city's perimeter.

Park, normally confident, sat sharpening her knife, silent.

And Lemma—

She stood apart from the group, arms folded, staring at the holo-model of the city's defensive grid.

Tanner stepped beside her.

"No turning back now."

She exhaled, nodding. "No. There isn't."

***

The attack began before they even had a chance to fully deploy.

"Explosions at the northern substation! They're hitting the grid!"

Tanner was already grabbing his rifle, moving fast toward the command tent exit.

"All teams, hold positions! Protect the shield nodes!"

The air shook as another blast erupted from the far side of the city. Plumes of smoke rose into the sky.

They're not just coming in waves. They're hitting everything at once.

Tanner sprinted toward the eastern defensive line, where Hale and Alvarez were already engaging hostiles pushing through a ruined district.

Gunfire flashed between the buildings, the narrow streets turning into bottlenecks of chaos.

"Hold the line!"

Hale was unloading rounds with brutal precision, cutting down enemy units as they surged forward.

"They're throwing everything at us, LT!"

Tanner dove behind cover, returning fire as he opened comms.

"Mercer, status on the shield activation?"

"Two nodes online! Third is under heavy fire!"

"We can't let them take it. If we lose a node before it syncs, the entire system collapses."

We have to push forward.

\*\*\*

Tanner signaled to Alvarez.

"We need to retake that node. Now."

Alvarez nodded. "I'll take a fireteam and clear the outer perimeter."

Tanner turned to Cooks and Park.

"You two, with me."

"We running or gunning?" Park asked, checking her rifle.

"Both."

They moved fast through the streets, dodging incoming fire as they cut toward the shield relay tower.

Ahead, they could see the Mana faction setting up explosives near the power couplings.

"They're trying to destroy it outright!"

Tanner raised his rifle.

"Not today."

The battle exploded as Eagle Eight engaged.

Park took the first kill, a clean shot through the visor of a soldier arming a charge.

Cooks moved with surgical precision, dropping another before he could react.

Tanner rushed in close, taking down two enemies in hand-to-hand combat before slamming their detonator into the dirt.

"Disarm it!" he called to Mercer over comms.

"On it!"

The moment stretched, each second feeling too long—

Then—

"Node secure! Shield grid remains stable!"

*\*\*\**

"They're falling back!"

Tanner heard the call through his comm, but he knew better than to celebrate early.

The Mana faction wasn't retreating.

They were regrouping.

A new wave crashed into the western perimeter, heavier than before. Armored units. Mechs. Heavy artillery.

"This is their last push!"

Tanner gritted his teeth, pulling his rifle tight against his shoulder.

"Then we push harder."

Eagle Eight moved as one, cutting through the enemy's flanks, forcing them into a brutal close-quarters battle.

Gunfire, shouting, the sharp ring of metal against armor—

Tanner fought with everything he had.

He saw Hale go down, briefly pinned before Alvarez pulled him free.

Park took a hit to the shoulder but kept moving.

Cooks was everywhere at once, dragging wounded back behind cover, her uniform streaked in blood— some hers, some not.

The shield nodes were online.

They just needed time.

Then—

The Explosion

A sudden concussive blast ripped through the battlefield.

Tanner had half a second to register it before the force hit him full-on, lifting his body off the ground.

Everything spun—

Then—

There was a sickening thud as his body slammed into a jagged rock.

Pain exploded through him, but it was distant, muffled under the rush of static in his ears.

Everything sounded far away.

His vision swam, blurred shapes and flickering shadows moving somewhere above him.

Then, a voice—frantic, urgent.

"Tanner!"

Cooks.

Her voice was close, but fading.

Tanner tried to move, tried to pull himself back into the fight, but his body wouldn't respond.

His vision darkened at the edges.

The last thing he saw before the world turned black—

The sky above him—

The shield flaring to life.

***

The battlefield trembled as the final shield node came online, sending a deep, resonating hum through the air. Sparks of energy rippled outward, a bright arc of electromagnetic force stretching across the city's skyline, forming the first visible wave of the Veil of Protection.

"It's working!" Mercer's voice cracked through the comms, filled with urgency. "The shield is syncing—just a few more seconds!"

The Mana faction, realizing what was happening, threw everything they had left into the fight.

The sky lit up with the final barrage—artillery rounds, energy blasts, and projectile fire aimed directly at the city's core.

"Brace for impact!"

The first rounds struck the shield—

And disintegrated.

The energy pulses warped and bent around the barrier, their lethal force neutralized before they could ever reach the city.

The attackers hesitated, weapons still raised, but their artillery continued to fail against the growing shield.

Then, all at once, the Mana forces began pulling back, their battle cries turning into frantic retreat orders as the realization sank in—they had lost.

"They're falling back!" Alvarez called over comms.

"Maintain defensive positions," Park ordered, shifting her weight against a half-shattered wall, clutching her wounded shoulder.

Hale, still leaning against a makeshift barricade, let out a ragged breath, his rifle lowering slightly.

"Damn thing actually worked."

***

Smoke and dust hung thick over the battlefield, the echoes of battle still ringing in the air. The shield hummed softly overhead, shimmering with a soft glow as it settled into its stable form.

Cooks moved fast, checking the wounded, issuing orders to the remaining medics as they scrambled to stabilize the most critical injuries.

"Anyone seen LT?"

No response.

Her gut clenched.

She spun, scanning the field, her eyes darting between the ruins, the bodies, and the fallen.

Then, she saw the impact zone.

A jagged pile of rubble and scorched stone—and something half-buried beneath it.

Her heart stopped.

"Mercer, Hale! Over here!"

She ran, shoving debris aside, her hands slick with dust and blood as she uncovered what she feared—

Tanner.

Unmoving.

A deep gash along his forehead, his breathing shallow.

"Damn it, LT, wake up!"

Cooks pressed two fingers to his neck—there. A pulse. Weak, but there.

"He's alive!"

Mercer and Hale reached them, their expressions grim but determined.

"We need to get him out of here." Cooks' voice was tight, her usual humor gone.

Park limped toward them, clutching her shoulder but refusing to sit still.

"Med evac's inbound. Just hold on."

Cooks exhaled sharply, brushing a streak of blood away from Tanner's temple.

You're not dying on me, Tanner.

As the medics rushed in, lifting him onto a stretcher, Cooks lingered, watching.

She had seen plenty of soldiers go down in battle.

But something about this—about him—

No. He's too damn stubborn to die now.

Above them, the shield stood strong, flickering faintly under the dimming sun.

The battle was over.

But for Tanner—

The fight wasn't done yet.

# CHAPTER 45

## AWAKENING

A dull, rhythmic beeping cut through the haze.

Tanner's body felt heavy like he was sinking into the deepest part of the ocean. Every attempt to move sent a dull, aching throb through his muscles like his nerves had forgotten how to fire properly.

Where am I...?

He forced his eyelids to flutter, the light above him blinding at first, but after a few moments, the brightness softened into the sterile white of a medical bay.

He blinked again. The ceiling. The steady hum of medical monitors. The antiseptic scent of sterilized air.

Then, movement beside him.

A familiar voice, edged with sarcasm but laced with something else—something softer.

"I was starting to think you just enjoyed making me worry."

Tanner turned his head slowly, muscles groaning in protest.

Cooks stood there, arms crossed, her usual sharp attitude present but muted. Her red hair was a mess, stray strands falling from the hastily tied ponytail, and her uniform was still stained with dirt and dried blood.

She looked tired.

And he had a feeling it wasn't just from the battle.

"Cooks..." His voice came out hoarse, barely a whisper.

She raised an eyebrow. "That's it? Just 'Cooks'? No dramatic comeback? No 'where the hell am I'?"

He exhaled, attempting a half-smirk. "Figured you'd tell me anyway."

She snorted, shaking her head. "Damn right, I will."

She stepped closer, arms still crossed, but there was something in the way her eyes scanned over him—a quiet assessment, making sure he was really there.

"You've been out for over a day. Took a hell of a hit in the blast—concussion, two cracked ribs, and enough bruises to make you look like a damn art project."

Tanner inhaled slowly, feeling the sharp pull in his ribs.

"Could be worse."

Cooks scoffed. "Oh, it almost was. You damn near got yourself killed."

His eyes flicked to her again. That edge in her voice. She was pissed—but it wasn't just frustration.

It was something else.

He let the silence stretch for a beat before speaking.

"You were there?"

Her expression shifted slightly, the sarcasm dimming for just a second.

"Yeah."

She didn't elaborate, but she didn't have to.

He could picture it. The battlefield. The chaos. The moment he got hit.

She must've been the first one to find him.

He tried shifting again, but a sharp pain lanced through his side.

He winced, and before he could even react, her hand was on his shoulder, steadying him.

"Don't be an idiot," she muttered. "You're not walking out of here yet."

Tanner smirked weakly. "Wouldn't dream of it."

She rolled her eyes, but there was no real annoyance there.

"Good. Because if you pull another stunt like that, I swear to god, LT, I'll tie you to this bed myself."

Tanner arched a brow, his voice dry. "Didn't know you cared that much."

For a moment, just a flicker of a second, she hesitated.

Then, with a smirk, she patted his shoulder—harder than necessary.

"Yeah, well, don't get used to it."

He chuckled, but it came out more like a ragged breath, his ribs protesting.

Damn. Everything hurts.

Cooks watched him for a moment longer, then exhaled.

"Get some rest, LT. You're not done healing yet."

She turned to leave, but Tanner caught her wrist—just for a second.

She paused.

"Hey." His voice was softer this time. "Thanks."

She looked at him, and for once, there was no sarcasm, no deflection. Just a quiet nod.

"Yeah. Anytime."

Then, with one last glance, she pulled away, walking out of the infirmary.

Tanner let his head sink back against the pillow, staring at the ceiling, letting his body relax for the first time.

The battle was over.

But something told him this was far from the last fight.

# CHAPTER 46

## FAREWELL TO A BROTHER

The sky was gray and heavy as if even the planet itself mourned. A sharp wind cut through the ceremonial courtyard just outside the main base, but no one flinched from the cold.

They stood in perfect formation, dressed in clean, pressed uniforms, the insignia of Eagle Eight prominent on their shoulders.

In front of them, a single metal casket rested on the raised platform, draped in a dark flag—not Earth's, not the local government's, but the insignia of their unit. A silent acknowledgment that Maddox had died not for one country, but for all of them.

Tanner stood at the head of the line, his ribs still tightly wrapped, his body aching from every step. But pain didn't matter. Not today.

Beside him, Cooks, Park, Mercer, Hale, Alvarez—all standing rigidly still, their grief masked by the stoicism drilled into them over the years.

But it was there.

In the set of Park's jaw.

In the way Mercer's fingers curled into a fist.

In the way Cooks kept her arms crossed too tightly.

The funeral was simple, as Maddox would've wanted it. No grand speeches or long-winded traditions—just a few words, a last goodbye, and then... nothing.

Julek stood at the side, a rare sign of respect from their alien allies. Even Ladrinen had come, though he remained silent, watching with an expression that was hard to read.

When it was time, Tanner stepped forward, clearing his throat before speaking.

"Maddox was the kind of guy who could make you laugh at the worst damn time. Not because he didn't take things seriously, but because he knew we had to—otherwise, we wouldn't get through half the shit we've been through."

He paused, glancing at the insignia on the casket.

"He was family. And we don't forget family."

Tanner stepped back, and without needing an order, Mercer and Hale lifted their rifles.

A three-volley salute cracked through the courtyard. The sharp echo of the shots rang in Tanner's ears long after the last casing hit the ground.

One by one, Eagle Eight approached the casket.

Park placed a worn playing card on top—the same deck Maddox used to hustle them in poker.

Cooks placed his old knife, the one he always claimed had "saved his ass more times than his rifle."

Hale muttered something under his breath, too quiet for anyone to hear, before placing a single bullet beside the others.

Then, as the sky darkened overhead, they stepped back.

The wind carried away the final echoes of the salute.

Maddox was gone.

But not forgotten.

# CHAPTER 47

## REFLECTION AND FALLOUT

Tanner sat alone in the dimly lit barracks, staring at the half-empty glass in his hands.

His body still ached from the battle, but the real pain—the one he couldn't shake—was something deeper.

Maddox was gone.

One of his own.

And no matter how much he tried to tell himself it was just part of the job, no matter how many missions they'd all signed up for knowing the risks…

It didn't make it any easier.

A soft knock at the door pulled him from his thoughts.

He didn't look up.

"Come in."

The door opened, and Cooks stepped inside, holding a bottle.

"Figured you'd be in here drinking alone like a jackass."

Tanner huffed a quiet laugh. "Not much of a party, I know."

She pulled up a chair across from him, setting the bottle down between them.

"You gonna keep blaming yourself for this?"

Tanner didn't answer right away.

"He was my responsibility."

Cooks sighed, leaning forward, resting her arms on her knees.

"Yeah, he was. And he knew that. And he trusted you. You think he'd want you sitting here drinking yourself into a hole?"

Tanner shook his head slightly, exhaling. "No."

"Then stop."

Her voice was softer than usual. Not an order. A request.

They sat in silence for a moment, the weight of the past few days hanging between them.

Finally, Cooks poured herself a drink, lifting her glass.

"To Maddox."

Tanner raised his own, their glasses clinking softly in the quiet room.

"To Maddox."

They drank.

Not to forget.

But to remember.

***

The next morning, Tanner stood in Ladrinen's office, the ambassador's expression tight with discontent.

"You disobeyed orders."

Tanner stood at attention, jaw clenched. "I did what was necessary."

Ladrinen's nostrils flared. "You're lucky the shield worked, or I'd be calling for your immediate dismissal."

"But it did work." Tanner met his gaze, unflinching. "And your people are still alive because of it."

Ladrinen exhaled sharply, running a hand over his ridged brow.

"You and your team are reckless, Lieutenant. Effective—but reckless."

Tanner didn't respond.

Ladrinen studied him for a long moment before finally speaking.

"I suppose I should be thanking you."

That caught Tanner off guard.

"Sir?"

Ladrinen sighed. "The city stands. My people live. That is not something I take lightly."

Tanner gave a short nod.

"Then let's make sure it stays that way."

Ladrinen's expression remained unreadable, but finally, he waved Tanner off.

"Dismissed, Lieutenant."

Tanner turned and exited, stepping into the cool corridor.

Outside, his team was waiting.

Hale stepped forward, "What next?"

Tanner took a slow breath, glancing at each of them before answering.

"Next? Home. We go home for now."

The team stood quiet for a moment, letting the words settle.

Then, without another word, they turned and walked together—toward whatever came next.

# ACKNOWLEDGMENTS

I would like to give a special thank you to my daughter, Emma, for her passion and enthusiasm for the book before I even began to write it.

I also would like to thank spell-check; my spelling is far from superior and spell-check keeps me on track.

# ABOUT THE AUTHOR

John lives in Georgia with his wife, two daughters and far too many animals. He enjoys Lego, SCUBA diving and just about everything tech.